10-Minute Stories From Ancient Rome

The Mighty Mortals Who Built the Greatest Empire the World has ever known.

Joy Chester

CONTENTS

Preface   V

Part I: Aeneas, the last Trojan   1

Chapter 1: The Wrath of Juno   3

Chapter 2: All at sea   9

Chapter 3: Dido, Queen of Carthage   16

Chapter 4: The Burning Ships and the Golden Bough   23

Chapter 5: The Coming of the Fury   30

Chapter 6: The Armor of Aeneas   37

Chapter 7: Evander and Pallas   44

Chapter 8: The Final Battle   51

Part II: The Etruscan Kings   56

Chapter 1: Romulus and Remus   58

Chapter 2: The Palatine and the Aventine   63

Chapter 3: The Sabine Women 69

Chapter 4: Numa and Ancus 76

Chapter 5: The Fall of the Last King 82

Part III: Hannibal – Rome's Worst Nightmare **88**

Chapter 1: Elephants in the Alps 90

Chapter 2: Defeats and Delays 97

Chapter 3: The Long Stalemate 104

Chapter 4: Zama & the Fall of Hannibal Part 110

IV: Julius Caesar **117**

Chapter 1: The Triumvirate 119

Chapter 2: The Die is Cast 126

Chapter 3. The Ides of March 134

Character Summary & Pronunciation Guide **141**

PREFACE

C hildren nowadays seem to read less and less. Reading a book can seem like a chore, when entertainment can be gained through a screen so much more easily. But studies have shown that developing an "atomic habit" - just doing ten minutes a day of whatever skill or habit you want to take on can be more than enough to engrain it into our lives. Therefore, we have transformed timeless, legendary stories into 10-minute, bite-size chunks, which are long enough to entertain, enthral, even educate the reader, but are short enough to be enjoyed quickly at bedtime or at any other point in our busy modern days. Within a matter of weeks, reading just 10 minutes a day, children can develop a habit which will benefit their lives immeasurably. It starts with just the turn of a page.

We return to the Mediterranean, beginning with Aeneas, whom we left just as he was escaping the burning of Troy by Agamemnon and his Greeks. Aeneas marked the end of the "Age of Heroes", but he has one more battle left to fight: it is his destiny, albeit distantly, to found Rome. Borrowing from the titan of Roman poetry, Virgil, as well as historians such as Livy, we present here a potted history of crucial points in the formation of the Roman state. What people don't often realize is that Rome had an empire long before it had an emperor. Scipio, Fabius, Flaminius, and hundreds of others like them built it long before Pompey, Crassus, and Caesar came on the scene. Even Octavian (who became the first true emperor, Augustus) only solidified things.

The Romans believed in (more or less) the same gods as the Greeks, but changed their names. Thus Zeus becomes Jupiter, Ares becomes Mars, Aphrodite becomes Venus, and Hera becomes Juno. Another thing to note is that, obviously, the Romans in this book lived before the time of Jesus, and thus dates in "years BC" would make no sense to them. They marked their years "ab urbe condita", from the founding of the city. Thus, a timeline has been included to help make sense of when (in our temporal understanding) these events happen.

Rome has given us some of history's most incredible characters, but it also built the ideas of statehood and politics which we hold to today. They wouldn't have understood democracy in the same way we do, but there was a sense of it. In the same way, they were comfortable giving individuals huge amounts of power, but were cautious of those who wanted too much! A careful balance was maintained, until the coming of the first triumvirate, when everything was turned on its head.

Each chapter can stand alone or be read in order. You could enjoy them at bedtime, in the car, on a plane, wherever you like. That's the magic of these tales, you can take them with you anywhere! Some of the more gruesome or difficult details have been left aside, lying ready in the original texts for the adventurous soul who wants to dive in, having been hooked by the gripping tales in this book. That's the hope, anyway, for these are some of the greatest stories ever told. There is a whole world out there, ready to be discovered.

As we have said before, dear reader: be ready to be thrilled, excited, scared, disgusted, confused, enthralled, and delighted. We truly envy you, because you are about to read these stories for the very first time, and that is a special moment. Take a deep breath and dive on in.

Part I

Aeneas,
the last Trojan

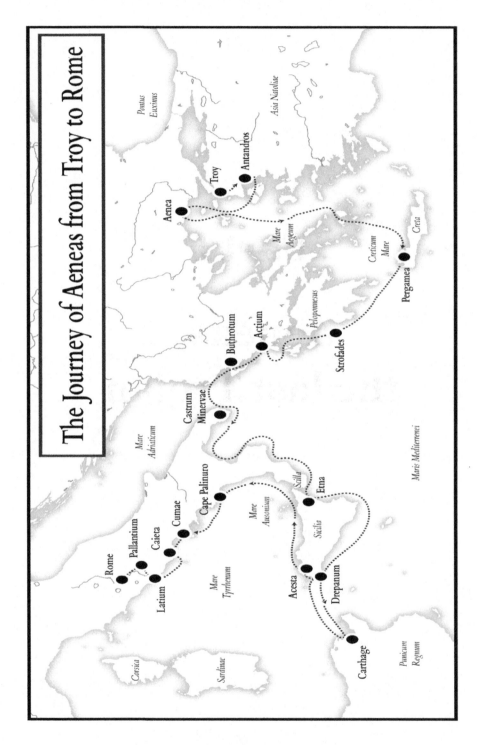

The Journey of Aeneas from Troy to Rome

CHAPTER 1: THE WRATH OF JUNO

Aeneas, prince of Troy, was homeless. Homeless and adrift on a dark sea where the stars were strange. At night he still woke in a cold sweat from dreams of fire and slaughter and loss. No matter how hard he tried, he could not clear his mind of the memories of Troy burning and of the cruel deaths of King Priam and countless others. For ten, long, hard years, the Greeks under Agamemnon of Mycenae had besieged Troy and the lands around. Many had fallen on both sides, even mighty Hector and indomitable Achilles.

But through a vile trick, the Greeks had taken Troy: wily Odysseus had built a great wooden horse, and left it and a liar, Sinon, behind on the shores of Ilium. Sinon had promised his service to Troy and convinced King Priam that the Greeks had finally gone for good, leaving the horse behind as an offering to the sea god Neptune. Priam had taken the horse inside his high-walled city, and as the Trojans feasted and sang, the Greeks had lain in wait. For the wooden horse was hollow, like Greek promises, and when all was quiet in the streets of Troy, the men who had hidden inside the horse's belly slipped out, killed the guards at the city gates, and let Agamemnon's army inside.

Aeneas had been awoken by the ghost of Hector himself, who had warned him of the Greek's treachery and told him to flee. Somehow Creusa, Aeneas' wife, had been slain in the confusion, and her ghost had come to him as he fought the desperate fight in the streets. She had echoed Hector's words that Aeneas would lead his people away from Troy and find a new life for them all in a faraway land called Italy, in a place where a river passed seven hills. Neither Aeneas nor his father Anchises had any idea in which direction they should sail, and thus the small Trojan fleet of just seven ships let the wind take them where it would.

High above on Mount Olympus, however, a fierce debate shook the home of the gods. Juno, queen of Olympus, had been singing with triumph at the fall of Troy, only to discover that not a few but a fleet of Trojans, under the command of prince Aeneas, had escaped the fire. Her hatred of these people had burnt hotly since Paris, son of Priam, had awarded Venus the golden apple as the most beautiful goddess instead of her. Now her anger, which all had thought long-gone, now blazed anew.

"We should smite him with thunder," she hissed, "blast him with hurricanes and shatter his wretched fleet, sending them to the depths of the sea."

The other gods and goddesses looked away from her. All were weary of fighting, for the Trojan War had lasted far longer than any mortal contest, and it had seen many of the greatest humans die over a single city. But then one of the immortals rose and stood before Juno. But it was not Mars, god of war, nor Minerva, goddess of wisdom. Even Jupiter, king of the gods, sat silent on his throne. It was Venus, goddess of love, who now opposed Juno, her long, golden hair crackling as her own emotions rose.

"Aeneas has done nothing to dishonor you," Venus said, her voice firm. "Throughout the long siege, he sacrificed and prayed to all the gods, even those who stood openly against the Trojans." She glanced around at Minerva, Neptune, and Vulcan, the god of smiths. They all nodded silently. "Troy has fallen, the Greeks are victorious. Your revenge for Paris' slight against your beauty, Juno, is surely complete. So do not pretend that this has anything to do with a golden apple. Why do you continue your pointless vendetta?"

With narrowed eyes, Juno turned upon the goddess of love, "And let us not pretend that your continued support of Aeneas is some honorable defense of the humble and weak! I know your secret, Venus: Aeneas is your son! You lay with a mortal, Anchises of Troy, and bore him a son!" Her tone was disgusted, but her eyes were triumphant.

A hushed muttering filled the room, as the other immortals turned to each other with wide eyes. Venus' beautiful cheeks flushed slightly, but she held her chin proudly and did not look away. "I do not deny it," she replied, "Aeneas is my son. But what of it? Is it not just and right that I protect and guide my own flesh and blood? But what of you, Juno? What is the source of your rage against the Trojans? Do you fear that they might achieve?"

Sparks flew from Juno's eyes, "Fear? I? I fear nothing. But the time of Troy has passed," here she turned to Jupiter, "Husband, do you not agree? The Trojans had their chance and the Greeks snuffed out their light. The strong rise and the weak are crushed underfoot.

So it is with all things. Our role as gods is to maintain this natural order, so that none try to outstay their time."

"Then whose time is it?" snapped Venus. But a look of sudden realization passed over her face. For a moment, it was as though the fog of morning had lifted from the sea and she could see clear across the waves. Not a single island nor rock was hidden from her. "Carthage!" Venus breathed, "You want Carthage to rise."

"Carthage?" asked Mars, frowning slightly, "that little town in Africa? You can't seriously think that..."

"Carthage has a great history before it!" shouted Juno, cutting across the war god, "it is perfectly placed on the northern coast to command the whole Mediterranean. The Carthaginians are led by a wise and noble queen, Dido, and she will be but the first of a long line of strong rulers whose shadows shall stretch far out from their home."

Venus could hardly believe her ears. Turning to Jupiter, hands on hips, she cried, "what of the fate decreed for my son, oh king of gods and men? Did the Fates themselves not decree that from him would rise a mighty people?"

All eyes turned to the king of the gods. He alone appeared calm and unmoved by the shocking revelations and high emotion echoing through his palace. Stroking his long, white beard, he regarded the two angry goddesses before him. "Both of you speak truthfully," he said, his deep voice quieting all mutters and murmurs as everyone held their breath to listen, "but even I do not ask the Fates how destiny will unfold. From the line of Aeneas a mighty empire will rise, but Carthage will also know greatness."

"And so, Dido will be cast aside, just because she is not of Aeneas' blood?" shrieked Juno, "What madness, what injustice now holds in the prophecies of the Fates? Is it because she is a woman? She has achieved far more than many a king, though he ruled twice as long as she."

A thunderous look from her husband silenced Juno, however, and the Olympian king continued, "Let everyone follow their own destiny. Fate runs like a river: You can throw a stone in, build a dam, even reroute its course, but it will eventually find the sea."

His pronouncement made, Jupiter rose and left the room. In pairs or singly, the other gods also left, until only Juno remained. Crossing to the window, she scowled at the endless stretches of land and sea, hidden in places by patches of cloud, "They will sing the song of Achilles and of Odysseus. Already the bards are strumming their harps and preparing their lyrics. They think that with Troy gone, the war can finally be over. But war never ends, it merely shifts location. The crows take wing and search for the next fires. So, while they sing of peace and of heroes go to their graves, I will sing anew, of weapons and of a man." Her knuckles were white on the window-ledge, and her eyes shone with a fierce light, "Aeneas, war is coming for you."

Down on the wide, wine-dark sea, the small Trojan fleet floated. Most of the survivors were young, but Anchises, father of Aeneas, was old and his hands lacked the strength they once had, but he was still wise. By right of age, experience, and bloodline, he should have been the one to lead the remaining Trojans. However, being wise, he knew that a new generation should take the reins, and thus he had watched with pride as his only son, Aeneas, led the survivors of

Troy away from their homeland in search of a new one. The choices that lay before them were difficult, and while he never spoke against his son in public, often would he advise him in private. So it was, as the sun set on another day of drifting over the waves, Anchises took his son aside and said, as gently as he could, "Aeneas, you have done much for our people, but we cannot drift like this any longer. A leader has to lead, actively lead. If you don't know where to go, then find a path to follow until you do."

A frown creased the handsome face of the young Trojan prince, "Neither of us knows where this place called Italy lies, and no merchant we have met can tell us either." Looking out over the sea, a small gasp left his lips as his eyes fell on a small island, a shadow on the horizon. "Perhaps the gods can give us more information!" he breathed, "Is that not Delos, home of the temple of Apollo?" Leaping to the helm, he heaved the ship around, calling to the rest of the fleet to follow.

CHAPTER 2: ALL AT SEA

The fleet of exiled Trojans had arrived at the sacred isle of Delos. Leaving the ships moored in a bay, Aeneas went alone up the precipitous slope to where Anchises recalled the temple had stood. An eager light shone in his eyes as he entered the deeper darkness of the temple. A single candle sat on the altar and Aeneas knelt before it, clasping his hands in his lap. Without warning, a voice reverberated gently through the inky blackness, "The last Trojan comes to Delos."

His heart hammered against his ribs and his voice shook, "You know me? Then you know why I have come: Where must I go? Where can I lead my people and find a home?"

There was not a breath of air, but the candle flickered. "Sail to your forebears' home, if happiness you seek; Your destiny is to roam, and never to be meek."

Breath caught in Aeneas' throat, as though a death toll had rung. "Are you saying that I shall never settle? That my people will never know peace?" But the voice did not reply. Bowing his head, he clenched his fists still tighter before rising to his feet. "Thank you, great god Apollo."

Anchises alone remained awake as his son returned to the ships. Even in the moonlight, he could see Aeneas' hands shaking. "A bad omen?" he asked, but even as he tried to keep his voice steady, his spirit quailed within him. "Did you at least learn where or what Italy is?"

Aeneas repeated the god's message. "I don't understand: how can we sail to our forebears' home? Troy has fallen and lies in ashes."

But a strange smile was spreading over Anchises' wizened face, "Troy was our home, Aeneas, but our family has not always lived there. My grandfather's grandfather was born in Crete. Perhaps Italy is a new name for that island!"

Excited, Aeneas gripped his father's hand, "Does Crete have seven hills?"

Anchises paused a long while, "It is now many years since I saw that southernmost island, and my memory fades. But I think it might."

Hope sprang again in Aeneas' heart, as a candle in the darkness. "Tomorrow," he said, his voice trembling, "we sail south and home."

Crete is the largest and most southernmost island in all of Greece. The great palace of Minos, who had ruled nearly a century before, still stood, but no one knew where to find the entrance to the fabled labyrinth, home of the monstrous Minotaur. The beast had been slain by the Athenian hero, Theseus, and Minos' fortunes had waned after that, and his people had dwindled. Thus, when the Trojans arrived, there were few inhabitants who even noticed their arrival. Those who protested took one look at the mighty figure of Aeneas and his war-scarred followers and quickly went away again.

Fields were planted, simple houses were built, and Aeneas could not help but smile as he watched hope brighten in his friends' eyes day by day. But as time went on, a shadow crept into their hearts. The crops failed or were meager; the few animals they had with them sickened and died; and even the Trojans themselves found themselves weakening, either from lack of good food or due to the same malady as afflicted the land about them. Aeneas went to their neighbors, but was turned away with cries of fear: no one wanted to risk infection, though as far as Aeneas could see, the Cretans' crops and livestock remained untouched.

Some of the Trojans argued that they should drive the Cretans away, take their land and their cattle and leave this cursed spot. But Aeneas disagreed, "If we act in this way, we shall be no better than the Greeks who drove us from our homeland. We must not be meek, but nor may we spread misery for our own gain." He looked around the land around them. Once it had looked so welcoming, but now every rock held an unfriendly feeling. "I am your leader still," he continued, "and a leader must be honest: I believe that we have made a mistake in coming to this island. The gods would not send such sickness on us if we were meant to be here. We must return to the ships and seek a new home."

Far above Crete, only two immortals noticed the Trojans setting sail: One was Venus who, despite her many duties, always kept an eye on her son's progress. Her heart ached to see him suffer so, but it also swelled with pride as she watched him grow as a leader and as a man. The other goddess whose attention was caught by the white foam on the prows of Aeneas' fleet did not hold such warmth for the exiled prince. Juno's heart had settled slightly when she had seen the Trojan walls rising on Crete. For a while she had hoped that perhaps Aeneas would never make it to Italy, that he would stay in the south. But now, as the seven ships sailed slowly westward, fear and hatred rose like twin pythons in her breast.

She dared not intervene herself, however, for she knew that Jupiter would punish her for going against his instructions. Therefore, she flew down to a small island far out in the middle of the sea. Clouds flocked around it like so many sheep; breezes and gusts flitted through the grass and whistled around her as she came to the door of a great house high on the cliffs. An old man with white, wispy hair and beard answered her knock. "Queen Juno!" he gasped, "I'm simply tripping over guests it seems. Why, Odysseus of Ithaca sailed away not ten days ago. I do hope he made it home, all the winds I trapped in that bag from him came back alright. Anyway, do come in." He bowed her inside, called for wine, and would have burst into further talk if Juno had not leaped into speech first.

"Aeolus, I need a favor from you."

The god of winds smiled more broadly, "What kind of favor, my queen?"

"The kind which is done quickly and quietly," replied Juno. "You know, I assume, that not all the Trojans died or were captured by Agamemnon and his forces? One band escaped and is wreaking havoc across the seas. Somehow, they have brought a blight down on the happy island of Crete and are now heading westwards, looking for new prey. I want them destroyed."

Aeolus' eyebrows raised, "And so you come to me? I'm flattered, my lady, but I have also heard that Jupiter himself has said "let Fate follow where it may". I do not think it wise to tempt fate or our king's wrath. I am sorry."

Juno put down her goblet. Rising to leave she smiled sweetly at the old god, "Of course I understand, dear Aeolus. I should have been more considerate. Neptune warned me that you are not the god I remember from the days of the Titan War, and much of your strength has left you. Perhaps he will aid me instead."

The goblet of wine went flying as a gust of wind knocked the table over. Aeolus' eyes blazed, "Not the god he remembers?" he cried. "Well Neptune seems to forget that while he may be the god of the sea, the sea is nothing without the wind!" Rolling up his sleeves, he dashed out of the house. Juno, her cruel grin broad on her face, followed. Already she could feel the air moving, sense the rage as the clouds darkened from white to grey and then to black. Bracing herself against the gusts, she watched with satisfaction as Aeolus marshaled the winds and sent them flying across the sea, faster than any eagle. "Let's see what you make of that, Neptune!" he howled.

Lightning struck the sea and thunder boomed overhead. Wind ripped sails to shreds and rain pelted down. Women and children desperately bailed water from the boats while the men heaved on ropes or oars. Aeneas stood like an oak at the helm, his eyes on the sky. "Gods above us and below," he cried, "do not let it end like this!" A great, green wave plunged over the side and deluged them all in icy water. Screams of fear were whipped away on the howling gale.

But down in his palace of coral and shells, Neptune, lord of the wide oceans, heard the tumult and the prayers of the terrified Trojans. Rising in wrath, he took up his mighty trident and struck the seafloor in his fury. "What ruckus is this?" Within moments his head broke the surface of the waves and he saw the miserable plight of the beleaguered ships. But he cared less for their fears than he was angered by the storm Aeolus had sent. "Aeolus may command you, but the sea is my realm!" he roared at the winds. A great storm cloud billowed above him and sought to envelop the sea god, but Neptune struck out with his three-pronged trident, slicing into the storm's very heart.

"Leave!" he boomed, deafening even the thunder. "I shall have peace here a while longer!"

Fearing his wrath, the winds fled, driving the clouds before them until blue skies shone where moments before all had been dark and doom-laden. Neptune watched them depart, and then sunk back into the waves without a glance at Aeneas and his people.

The Trojan fleet had somehow survived. Several men and women had been lost to the waves, and the ships themselves were barely staying afloat. To the west, land could be seen and, exhausted as they were, all lent a hand to row to shore. Having survived the storm, there was in the hearts of all a bright spark of hope. All but Aeneas. His proud head was bowed, and tears flowed freely, for in the midst of the horror and terror of the storm the great heart of Anchises had failed. Thus, while the Trojans rowed slowly towards the unknown land, their prince clutched his son to his chest and mourned his father. And high up on Mount Olympus, Venus shed bitter tears for the mortal man she had once loved.

Chapter 3: Dido, Queen of Carthage

Having barely survived Aeolus' storm, Aeneas and the Trojans buried his father, Anchises, on the shore of Libya. They sang sad songs and wept long, for all had loved the old man. Once the funeral rites had been completed, Aeneas shouldered his shield and led his men to the high-walled city they had seen from the sea. "If I am right," the prince told his men, "This city is called Carthage."

He was correct, and the Carthaginians welcomed the Trojans gladly. Queen Dido herself came to the front steps of her palace and ushered the tired men inside. "And you must send for the rest of your people, too!" she insisted, seating Aeneas beside her. "Tales of the great war at Troy have reached even here. But fear not: We have no alliance with the Greeks."

Encouraged as much by her kindness as by the beauty of her eyes, Aeneas gladly accepted a cup of sweet wine and began the story of the final days of Troy, of their desperate flight from the burning city, and of their hard journey since. Dido sat enthralled by their adventures, and when Aeneas' eyes filled with tears as he came to the death of his own father, she clasped his hand in hers. "We are honored that so great and famous a man has found his final resting place on our shores."

Aeneas bowed his head and then rose. "Thank you, but where is the king? The hour grows late and yet I have not had a chance to thank our host for his company."

A shout of laughter rose at his words, and Aeneas stared around him in confusion and not a little anger. But then Tyrian, a noble of Carthage stood and clapped the Trojan prince on the shoulder. "Let your brows unfurl, great-hearted Aeneas. We are not laughing at you, really. The truth is Carthage has no king. We are honored that Queen Dido led us here from Tyre. Not so long ago, we were fugitives like you, but thanks to the courage, strength and, I will say, the shrewdness and wisdom of Dido, we have made this place our home."

Aeneas' eyebrows raised, and he made swift apologies to the queen, who waved them away.

"You have achieved much, great Queen, in so short a time. Your walls have already risen high!" said Aeneas, casting a marveling glance around the beautifully carved columns and the great doors.

"But you don't even know the half of it!" laughed Tyrian, his barrel-like chest bursting with pride. "This land once belonged to Iarbas, a powerful ruler, but also a brute and a bully. When we first came here, we had so little gold that Iarbas was barely willing to give us anything. But our queen was cunning and begged him to give us as much land as she could fit inside an ox hide. Well, Iarbas laughed and had one of his prize bulls butchered and skinned that day. 'Here,' he said, 'this was the biggest in my herd. Place it wherever you like!' And so, Dido took a knife and cut the hide in such an intricate, looping way that it made a vast circle of leather so thin a spider would have been proud to build its web from it!"

"Tyrian!" laughed Dido, "You exaggerate, as ever!"

But Tyrian plowed on, "Thus it was that she laid out the vast ring and it contained all this land on which our fair city now stands! Iarbas was at a loss for words, but he had promised, and he feared the gods too much to go back on his word. I doubt that even that artful schemer Odysseus could fail to be impressed with our noble queen's mind! Therefore, great Aeneas, we are proud to be the only city in the world that bows its knee only to a queen. For with such a queen as Dido, what need do we have for a king?"

In the weeks that followed, Aeneas and Dido spent much of their days together. They would ride out across the fields around Carthage or walk through the city's scented gardens. Seeing them together, an idea came to Juno, queen of Olympus. For Carthage was her city, and she knew that Aeneas' line was destined to rule the greatest city in the world. "But," she wondered, "what if Aeneas chose to stay here? Then fate itself shall be re-written and Carthage would stand above all!" Flushed with excitement, she rushed to Venus, Aeneas' mother and suggested the alliance. "We have argued before," said Juno coaxingly, "but why not lay that aside? I am sorry for the harm done to Aeneas thus far, but that would all be in the past. Apollo sings songs of the Age of Heroes, but I recall only the death and destruction. Let Dido and Aeneas join their destinies together, and imagine what they and their descendants could achieve? Think of it: an age of peace."

Venus smiled at Juno but was not deceived by her honeyed words. "Fate cannot simply be smoothed over like sand and etched anew," she thought. "And besides, Aeneas' descendants will be greater than

Dido's. Jupiter himself has told me so!" Keeping these thoughts to herself, however, Venus nodded, "I shall not oppose your plan." Juno's eyes sparkled, and both goddesses went their separate ways with triumph leaping in their hearts.

And so, Juno whispered in Dido's ear, and the queen felt love and joy in every moment she spent with the Trojan prince. But the same could not be said for Aeneas. Juno would often hiss thoughts of marriage into his mind and skip away, convinced her scheme was proceeding as planned. But always Aeneas would brush them aside, never realizing that the queen of the gods herself was their source. "I have a destiny to fulfill," he reminded himself dutifully whenever these thoughts rose unbidden within him. Thus, there came a day when Aeneas went to Dido and announced that he must leave Libya and sail on. "I have a duty to my people and a destiny to follow," he explained, not noticing the way Dido's face was going white with shock. "I thank you for your kind hospitality, but our home does not lie on your shores."

"You thank me?" cried Dido, her heart seeming to split in two in her chest. "After all the time we have spent together, that is all you have to say to me?" Aeneas backed away slightly, confused and stunned at her reaction.

"Dido, I assure you..."

"Be silent, you snake!" she shrieked, "I should have known that you were only using me, growing fat on our wine and food. You deceptive, vile beast! Leave! Sail away and may your shadow never darken my door again!"

In the shining halls of Olympus, Juno watched Aeneas' departing fleet with wrath coursing through her veins. And just as the queen of the gods raged, so too Dido hurled herself around the fine corridors of her own palace. Few dared to look at her, and those who did drew away in terror at what they saw. For it was as though she had been possessed by some terrible spirit. She clawed at her hair and tore her gown. Screaming at the maids to collect everything Aeneas had ever touched: bedsheets, chairs, plates; she built a great pyre in the courtyard. Even the nobles of her council, brave men who had sworn their lives to the queen cowered in fear at her staring eyes. "It is as though Pluto, lord of the Underworld, has sent an avenging Fury to Carthage!" whispered Tyrian.

Quietly though he had spoken, Dido heard him. "Truly, I am a Fury!" she cried, "but not sent to Carthage, rather sent for it." She seized a burning torch from the wall and tossed it onto the pile of splintered wood and assorted items. Smoke wreathed about her like storm clouds building around a mountain's slopes. In the blazing light of the fire, her eyes shone red. "What I shall do tonight," she screamed, "can never be undone! This I call the gods themselves to witness: Firstly, I swear that Carthage shall never bow to a foreign ruler."

The hairs on the heads of the watches rose, and they shivered despite the heat from the pyre.

"Secondly, I curse Aeneas the Trojan. Whatever land he finds himself shall give him no joy. He must fight every day of his life! And thirdly, from this night henceforth, our cities shall ever be opposed. No son or daughter of Carthage may forget what is done this day nor have any greater enemy than those who come from Aeneas' line. This I vow with my life's blood!"

Too late, Tyrian realized what Dido had in mind. Even as he leaped forward to save his queen, she leaped high onto the blazing pyre, her torn clothes catching fire like a torch. A blade flashed in her hand and with a final cry, Dido plunged it into her chest.

The fire's crackling and hissing seemed choked by the deadly silence that followed. Finally, one of the guards managed to find his voice, "What do we do now?"

Tyrian turned away from the fire, his own eyes now burning like coals, "We never forget, never forgive. Dido is gone, but Carthage remains. Strong it is, but mighty it shall become. We shall build our navies, train our armies, until comes the day when there shall be no rock under which the kin of Troy may hide."

Chapter 4: The Burning Ships and the Golden Bough

The shoreline of Lybia fell behind the Trojan fleet. The next day brought a great island into view, and there, on its northwesternmost spur, they moored their ships and rested. For even Aeneas had to admit that he was not sure where they should sail next. Since the tragic loss of his father Anchises, he had felt uncertain and confused. So, while their prince studied maps and consulted his counselors, the last men and women of Troy busied themselves as best they could.

But over the hearts of all there loomed a shadow. Like dark clouds passing in the night, or the whistling of wind that hints and the howling of wolves, unease turned to fear and then even to dread. To one woman, Ctimene, it seemed that her concern for her husband and her children stood at the door of her tent like a stern woman. "She reminds me of my mother-in-law," she said to herself, "or my old teacher perhaps. She comes only in my dreams and stands there, staring at me, like I am some naughty child who has strayed. But I know not what I have done wrong."

Ctimene did not tell anyone about her dreams, even when they continued to plague her. But they were no phantoms of her mind. For Juno, queen of the gods and enemy of the Trojans, stalked the camp. Like a snake she came unseen, hissing in unwary ears and bringing a silent disquiet to these people who had already suffered so much. Then there came a night without a moon, and Juno came again to Ctimene as she slumbered, one arm caressing her son.

"For years, it seems, you have sailed," Juno whispered to the sleeping woman, "having left so many friends behind. How many more has Aeneas lost along the way? He doesn't even know where he is going! But I do not blame him. Men are simple creatures. Give them a sword and they will kill. Give them a plow and they will grow crops, rich and filling. Give them a ship and they will sail beyond the end of the world. Give them a home, and they will bring you happiness. But when will you women have your say? When will you stand and cry 'Enough!'? When will you do what is necessary for your children and your grandchildren to come?" Ctimene, still sleeping, gasped as the tall, harsh, beautiful woman pulled back the tent flap to show her fields of golden corn through which dark-haired children danced and laughed, their fathers leaning on their tools and watching with proud eyes.

Her mind still hazy from sleep, Ctimene rose from her bed and took a burning brand from the fire. One of the guards at the edge of the camp watched her curiously as she headed down to the beach, but assumed, wrongly, that she needed something from the ships.

Only when the smoke wafted up to where he stood did he realize his mistake. "Fire at the ships!" he cried, tossing his weapons aside and calling to his fellows before hurtling down to the shore. Wood stained with tar and dried by sea salt burns quickly, and Ctimene had already set fire to half the fleet.

The guard managed to pull her away before she could finish her task, but already the flames were high above their heads. Aeneas, running like a deer, skidded to a halt before them as the men desperately tossed buckets of water over the burning ships. "Why?" he cried, the terror in his eyes matching the rage in hers. "Why burn our way forward?"

"Because there is no way forward!" Ctimene shrieked. "This island is fertile and empty. Why must we always look to the horizon, when we have found a perfectly good home right here? My children need solid earth beneath their feet, not the ever-shifting boards of boats!"

Seeing that some god had brought madness upon her, Aeneas turned away. The heat from the flames was terrible, and he raised his eyes to the heavens. No stars shone down, but still he prayed. "Great Jupiter, father of gods and men, if ever we have shown you due honor, save us now: bring rain and douse these flames!"

"Don't waste your breath!" Ctimene shouted, "The gods have long forsaken us!"

The woman's derisive cry was silenced by the fall of the first raindrop. Within moments, the clouds above were hurling down torrents of water, driving back the flames, leaving behind blackened boards and the burnt remnants of sails and ropes.

Aeneas turned back to Ctimene but was aware that all the Trojans on the beach were listening. "I don't know what dark dream drove you to such folly, but surely you see now that the gods have not forgotten us. Tomorrow I shall have our final voyage in mind. If you wish to stay, I will not beg you to continue."

Lying inside his tent, the rain still beating hard against the canvas, Aeneas tossed and turned, trying to decide in which direction they should sail next. Exhausted from fear and fatigue, he lapsed into uneasy dreams. He dreamt that he was walking through a dark forest. Ahead of him strode a young man whose skin shone like starlight. A wide-brimmed hat topped his golden curls, and his sandals had tiny, feathery wings, which flapped lazily as he strode along. "Mercury!" called Aeneas, "Messenger of the gods! Have you come to help me?"

But the god only smiled over his shoulder and walked on. As Aeneas blundered after him, he thought he saw a light, like that of the god, but golden. Out of the gloom loomed an ancient, twisted tree, so bent with age that the prince half expected it to fall over, from which grew a single golden branch. Mercury stopped nearby and gestured to it.

"Take the bough, if you can."

Aeneas glanced between the god and the tree. "What do you mean, 'If I can'?"

"Well, if you can't, then you'll wake up, and your journey will end here. But if you can, then you shall go down the darkest path to where the brightest light awaits you."

Sensing that he had no choice, Aeneas grasped the branch in both hands. It felt as though it was truly made of gold and, with a single tug, he tore the branch away.

"So it is to be," remarked the messenger of the gods and, with a whooshing of his winged sandals, he took flight. "Follow the bough until you find your guide," he called and disappeared into the gloom.

Aeneas stared up at where the god had disappeared, but it was useless calling after him. So, he raised the golden branch and strode forward, unsure if this was the way he had come or not. For what seemed an eternity, Aeneas walked on through this forest of never-ending night, until he saw a figure slowly materializing out of the darkness. Continuing without fear, he saw that it was a woman who was neither old nor young. "Are you a goddess?" he asked, but she shook her head.

"I am the Sybil." And, as though that was explanation enough, she turned and led him down a slope. Up until now, the land had been forested but flat. Now, however, Aeneas had to take care not to fall and drop his precious branch as the ground dropped away before him. With a swift intake of breath, he realized that the few nightbirds he had heard during his journey before had now all quietened or flown away. What few stars that were visible above them vanished, and Aeneas was dimly aware that they had stepped underground.

The sloshing of water now met his ears, and, by the soft glow of the golden bough, they saw a long line of people, grey and quiet, standing on the bank of a river. A single boat was moored at the bank with a ferryman so ancient that Aeneas wondered how he was still standing. Then his blood ran cold. "Charon!" he gasped. "The ferryman of the dead! But surely it is not my time to pass into Pluto's realm?"

"For the sake of destiny, you must," explained the Sybil, "Show Charon the golden bough, and he shall let you cross."

Aeneas doubted this would work, but indeed the old man was entranced by the bough's beauty. Without taking his eyes from the tender, shining leaves, he rowed them slowly over the black river, in which no reflection of light could be seen. The chill air caught in the Trojan prince's lungs, and it took twice as much effort to step out of the boat as it had to step in. Far ahead of them stretched the endless plains of the realm of Pluto, king of the Underworld. Here and there drifted the quiet shades of long-dead souls. Some eyes, grey and bleary, passed over Aeneas and the Sybil as they stumbled through the mist-strewn land.

Amongst the dead there were many faces whom Aeneas thought he knew: Fellow Trojans who had died in the war, or Greeks he himself had slain. But then there came a face which he knew better than any other: Anchises, just as wrinkled and care worn as the day he had died, sat by a small, silent pool.

"Father!" Aeneas' voice seemed muffled by the endless fog. "Father, I am here!"

The ghost of the old man looked up and managed a weak smile, "Thank the gods," he muttered, and his words seemed just to flit past his son's ears, as though he were speaking from far away. "We have little time. But know this, Aeneas: We were not wrong when we listened to the oracle at Delos. You must go to the land of our forefather."

Aeneas was confused, "But Teucris, your grandfather's grandfather, came from Crete. We tried going there and were driven away by plague."

"Yes," agreed his father's shade, "but we have more than one ancestor who traveled from afar to help found Troy. Dardanus ruled Italy's western shores long ago."

"Italy?!" cried Aeneas, and the bough in his hands seemed to dim in comparison to the light that cleared the mists from his mind."

With a gasp of wonder and joy, Aeneas awoke. Glancing down at his hand, he saw that he no longer held the golden bough, but his eyes shone in the pale morning light. "Finally, my path is clear before me!"

CHAPTER 5: THE COMING OF THE FURY

"How could this happen?" Juno raged. The queen of the gods had done everything she could to stop Aeneas, the last of the Trojan princes, from reaching Italy. She did not care about the promise Jupiter had made to Venus. As far as she was concerned, the Trojans should be wiped from the face of the earth and everyone should simply accept that Carthage, her beloved city, would rise to power and glory. "The time of Greece is coming to an end," she muttered, glaring out the window. "Soon a new empire shall rise to cloak the Mediterranean. That empire shall be Carthage!"

It was then that a cold, damp breeze whispered over her. The candles hanging from the ceiling dimmed. "I can smell the Stygian swamp on you," said Juno, wrinkling her nose and turning to face her visitor. "Why has Pluto sent you from the Underworld, Allecto?" Before her stood an old woman with grey skin that had never seen the sun, black, lank hair that had never been clean, and a face that had never smiled. In her hand there was a terrible black whip, hooked and barbed. She was one of the three Furies, the terrible jailors of Pluto, king of the Underworld, and his most vicious servants. Although Cerberus, the three-headed hellhound kept the souls within the gates, it was the Furies whom all feared to meet.

"My master has not sent me anywhere," hissed Allecto, "it was you that summoned me, great Queen of Olympus which splits the sky."

Juno stared at her for a long moment and then nodded, "Not in words, perhaps, but in my heart. There is work for you in the mortal world, Allecto. I wish to punish Aeneas, the last scion of Troy, for daring to escape his fate for so long. You must sow war between the Trojans and the peoples of Italy. I want so many to die that Aeneas will rue the day he dared step foot on Italian soil and challenge the inevitable rise of Carthage!"

Allecto's eyes narrowed, but she nodded. With the screech of metallic claws on the beautiful, glazed floor, she was gone.

Ascanius, son of Aeneas, crept through the undergrowth, bow in hand. After so long onboard the ship, it was a joy to finally have come to their journey's end. When the camp had been erected, Ascanius had begged his father to let him go with the hunting party. "I practiced lots in Carthage!" he had said, proudly showing his father his short bow and well-feathered arrows. "I'll bring back meat for dinner!" Aeneas had ruffled his son's hair and given his blessing but had quietly told the hunters to keep an eye on him. "This land will be our home, but we don't know it well, yet."

Now Ascanius's heart was thudding with excitement, for he had seen what none of the others had noticed: the small, shapely prints of a young deer. Somewhere off to his left, a noisome smell told him that a swamp was near. "The deer will stay clear of that," he told himself and pressed onwards. A shadow passed through the trees before him, and he held his breath as he tiptoed in pursuit. Then, his eyes widened as he saw it, a beautiful red coat with dapples of gold across its back. Taking a firm stance with his back straight, he aimed and fired. With a graceful sigh the deer slumped down, the arrow in its chest. Ascanius whooped with triumph, his cry bringing the other hunters to him. Seeing his prize, they clapped their hands on his shoulders and shook his hand. "We may have taken larger prey," said their leader, Pandarus, "but you have claimed the most beautiful. And what a shot, clean through the heart! Your father will be proud."

And so Aeneas was. He had not expected his son to hit more than a few tree stumps on his first expedition, but for the first time in longer than anyone could remember, the Trojan leader laughed as he saw his son's prize. "If only your grandfather were here to see it," he said, lifting Ascanius onto his knee. "He would have been as proud as I am. We shall eat well tonight!"

It was then that a shadow seemed to pass over the boy, just a fleeting look of doubt or worry, or like when a vulture flying high above passes over, and one only realizes that its silhouette was there when it is already gone. But when the moment passed, the brightness of his eyes was just as it had ever been. "Father, it is a beautiful deer, so beautiful that we should not waste it on a simple meal. Tomorrow you said you would go to the nearest town and speak with their king, Latinus. Why not take the golden deer as a gift?"

"A good shot with your bow and your mind!" grinned Aeneas, "It shall be as you say!"

In the nearby city of Latinum, the wise old king, Latinus, was in doubt. His only daughter, Lavinia, was already of marrying age, and yet he did not wish to see her go from his halls. Such was his turmoil that he had even asked the oracle of the gods for their advice. Their response had left him in a worse plight than before, for the gods had said that his daughter must marry a foreigner. Immediately, Turnus of the Rutulians had offered himself. "He's a brute!" screamed Lavinia, and Latinus could not disagree. But Turnus was also powerful, and an alliance would be good for the Latins.

The king's thoughts were interrupted by a messenger, "My king", the young man stammered, "A delegation of Trojans has come."

Latinus stared at the man, quite convinced that he had misheard, "Trojans? Don't be silly, boy. Agamemnon of Mycenae destroyed that city. There are no more Trojans."

The messenger shrugged, "That was the message, my lord, shall I tell them to leave?"

"No! No matter who they say they are, they are our guests. Jupiter would send plagues if we dared break the sacred law of hospitality."

But when Aeneas entered his hall, even Latinus had to stop himself from staring. To his right sat his wife, Queen Amata, and to his left was Lavinia. Both women gasped at the sight of Aeneas, for he was unlike any man they had seen before. While the men of Italy were strongly made and dark of hair, with fine noses and olive skins, Aeneas was no less well built, but he stood taller than any man they had seen, his auburn hair hanging in gentle ringlets. But it was his eyes that drew them most of all. In them, Amata saw the look of a man who long suffered. To Lavinia, they were the eyes of pure kindness. This man was both a father and a leader, and gave each equal care.

But Latinus, being older and with a longer memory, saw the eyes of a man whom he had once known. Rising to his feet, he clasped Aeneas by the forearm, as was the custom in Italy, and greeted him warmly. "The laws of Jupiter demand that first I welcome you into my home, give you food and wine, and only then ask your name. But I need not wait, for I already see the resemblance. The words of my messenger are true: You are from Troy. You are the son of Anchises, whom I once met long ago when he had been sent by King Priam to find his long-lost sister, Hesione. Where is he? For it would please me greatly to speak with him again."

Aeneas bowed his head in gratitude and sadness, "My father died, wise king, not so long ago. We mourn him still."

"It is right that you should, but leave your sadness at the door for a little while."

At that moment, the messenger scurried in again, and whispered in Latinus' ear. The old king sighed, "This timing is unfortunate, but I cannot deny him entry. Bid Prince Turnus enter." Aeneas turned to see a thick-set warrior with dark brows and a grim expression marching towards him. "Hail, King of Latinum!" Turnus bowed to Latinus, who smiled as best he could. "And who are you, stranger?" barked the Rutulian, turning on Aeneas who did not step back.

"He is Aeneas of Troy, my guest!" replied Latinus sharply, "We were just about to welcome these honored travelers with a feast. Would you join us?"

"I will," replied Turnus, "Any chance to sit with the beautiful Lavinia!"

The princess recoiled slightly but was relieved when Queen Amata bid the Rutulian to sit beside her. Another seat, next to Lavinia, was set for Aeneas, and soon wine and choice meats were brought forth.

Throughout the meal, both father and daughter plied Aeneas with questions, and Aeneas told his tales gladly, trying not to notice how Turnus' florid face was reddening still deeper with sullen resentment.

As the Trojan prince finished recounting his duel against Idomeneus on the banks of the Scamander, Lavinia turned to her father and cried, "Such bravery and skill, father, is he not wonderful, and a foreigner too!" Until that moment, the old man had sat with his brows furrowed in shadowy thought, but at his daughter's words a startled but joyful look rose on Latinus' face.

"Indeed he is," replied the old man. "The gods themselves seem to have ordained your coming, Aeneas. It has been foretold that my daughter must marry a man from foreign lands: would you be that man?"

Turnus leaped to his feet, but Latinus held his hand high. Aeneas rose also and bowed his gratitude, "Good king, I came in the hope of friendship, not of union. But if the gods themselves will it, I shall not refuse so kind an offer. It is fortuitous that I have brought a gift befitting such a joyful occasion." Beckoning to Ascanius, he continued speaking. "It so happens that yesterday my own son shot a deer in the woods so beautiful that it must have been put in his path by some divine power for this very moment."

The boy heaved the golden-dappled deer onto the table before the king and bowed, smiling from ear to ear.

But Queen Amata screamed. Turnus roared in fury. And even Latinus clutched at his heart, averting his eyes from what lay before him.

"This is what you would replace me with?" bellowed Turnus, hurling his chair aside. "If the gods themselves did not forbid it, I would slay you in this hall, Trojan dog! The insult of handing Lavinia to this barbarian was bad enough, Latinus, but now he offends the gods themselves?"

Aeneas gripped his sword but did not draw it. "What is this?" he cried, "What is wrong?"

Queen Amata pointed at the deer and gasped, "It is from the herd sacred to Diana, goddess of the hunt."

Turnus pointed at Aeneas and spat, "You may have come here in peace Aeneas, but you leave at war! Your blood shall cleanse these lands of this blasphemy!"

CHAPTER 6: THE ARMOR OF AENEAS

Aeneas wondered how it could all have gone so wrong so quickly. They had finally made it to Italy, the place promised by the gods as a safe refuge for him and his people. How his heart had sung when they had pulled their boats up onto the golden shore for the last time. But within days of arriving, they had visited King Latinus to make a potential alliance. Latinus had been so taken with Aeneas that he had even offered his daughter in marriage. But a well-intentioned gift from his son, Ascanius had shattered any chance of peace. By some terrible accident of fate, the boy had shot a sacred deer, and now the bad-tempered prince of the Rutulians, Turnus, was calling his allies and marshaling his troops.

There was one, very small comfort to be had: Latinus refused to march against Aeneas. "I am too old for war," the wizened king had said, ignoring the furious stare of his wife. "And I do not for a moment believe that you slew that deer on purpose. But I also see that some dark fate is closing in about you, son of Anchises. My men will not fight, but nor will I anger my neighbors and my friends by taking up arms in your favor. You must find allies yourself or, and it pains me to say it, leave before more innocent blood is split."

Therefore, Aeneas had taken his son by the hand, promised him that he was blameless in the whole affair, and returned with him to the Trojans' camp. There he had ordered the men to break up some of the ships and build strong walls. "What cruel irony it is," he had remarked, "that for ten years the Greeks camped thus on our gentle shores and now, after all our suffering, we are doing much the same thing. But we come not as invaders, and the gods are with us. In their promise I lay all our hopes."

But Aeneas knew, too, that the walls and strong arms of his fellow Trojans would not be enough to save his people and mark out a new home for them in this wide, fertile land. Latinus had sent word that Turnus was touring the neighboring lands, raising support for his war, and so Aeneas took one of his remaining ships and set sail. But he did not strike out to see, nor up the coast as many expected him to. "The gods told us that our future home lies where a river passes seven hills," he told his crew. "So, we shall sail inland, and find what help we may."

The river they now sailed up was wide and deep. Aeneas stood at the stern, his hand upon the tiller. The wind blew them steadily forth, and as night crawled over them most of his men slept. Thus, it was that Aeneas was alone when Father Tiber came. The prince did not see him climb aboard, but there he was, a tall man with reeds in his hair and beard. "It's about time you got here, son of Anchises," his voice was slow and deep, like the river itself. "I bid you welcome."

"Who are you, great god?" asked Aeneas, bowing his head respectfully.

Father Tiber smiled, "I am Tiber, and this is my river. I helped shape the land past which you now sail, but until you came, no-one ever wanted to be here. Men and women lived here, they grew and multiplied, but you are the first to strive through storm and tumult with this land as your prize. For that I am grateful. And so, I will grant you safe passage and give you some good advice: Go to Evander, king of the Arcadians. He is wise and kind and has no love for Turnus."

"Thank you, Father Tiber!" cried Aeneas. Reaching for his pouch, he pulled out a beautiful ring as a gift of thanks, but the god had already disappeared. "My people will honor you forever, great river," he whispered and, kissing the ring, he dropped it into the water.

Father Tiber was not the only immortal abroad that night. Venus, goddess of love and mother of Aeneas, strode the banks of the Tiber wreathed in mist. She watched her son as he sailed his ship confidently through the night. Rising onto a breeze, she surveyed the lands around, north, south, and east. A bird on the wing would have seen nothing, but even in the dark Venus could sense the rage of the Rutulians spreading like lava from a volcano. Slowly it was rolling across the land, gathering heat and power as it came. Soon enough that crimson tide of hate and fear would turn towards the Trojans, the one island of peace. Her heart shook within her. "I have stood by long enough," she said, "Juno has played her hand well. Even I cannot see how she has lit the fires of war any more than I can lay the blame for the dreadful storm at her door. But Aeneas needs more than my support and the promises of Jupiter, father of gods and king of men. He needs aid. He needs a weapon."

Swift as thought she flew south to Sicily. There, on the easternmost edge of the island, stood the mighty bulk of Etna. Some said that Typhon, the most terrible of all calamities and the greatest enemy of the Olympians, had been buried beneath that mountain. But the fury of that dread beast could never be fully contained, and thus Etna spewed fire and burning rock from its summit, shaking the island itself whenever Typhon turned in his caged slumber. There, in the center of the volcano's core, Vulcan, smith of the gods, had built his greatest workshop and forged Jupiter's thunderbolt, Neptune's trident, and Pluto's pitchfork.

Entering the scorching hot cavern, the walls of which danced with flickering red and gold, Venus squinted through the smoke to where the hunched figure of the smith-god was bent over a wide workbench, a tiny hammer and chisel in hand. As the goddess neared, he straightened, as best he could, revealing a tiny golden bird. With a wave of his hand, he dismissed it, and the beautiful metal creature flitted away circling Venus once, twice, three times before zooming out into the night. She had barely opened her mouth to speak when Vulcan interrupted, turning his ugly, twisted face upon her. Unlike the rest of the gods, Vulcan was not blessed with eternal beauty. But while Mars, god of war, was a mighty male paragon, his domain was the most hideous the world knew. Vulcan may not have been good-looking, but the fruits of his hands brought tears of joy even to Pluto, the dark lord of the underworld.

"I know why you have come, Venus. You wish me to make armor for your son. Well, I have had my fill of war. I made Achilles a glorious shield and a bright blade, and within a week he was dead. What does that say about my creation?"

Venus rested a shapely hand on Vulcan's broad shoulder, "Achilles was fated to die at Troy, my son is fated to live and bring about the greatest empire the world will ever see. But he needs your help. Juno is marshaling the forces of Italy against him, and I fear what will happen if she succeeds. And do not forget: Aeneas' story will last for thousands of years. But you can forge in metal something that no words can ever equal. When Aeneas treads the field, it will not be the fury of Mars that the poets will tell of, but rather the radiance of his armor and the beauty of his sword. Let that be your legacy to the world, master smith."

Grimy tears formed in the ash-strewn face of the god of smiths. "This shall be my last work of war," he said, turning to his bellows, "and it shall be my greatest, I promise you. The age of heroes ended at Troy, they say. But my armor will remind the world that one last hero still walks the earth."

Venus could only watch in awe as he worked. Tireless as a river, swift as lightning, the mighty smith heaved on the bellows and hammered the white-hot metal. A great round shield, a peerless sword, a high-plumed helm, and a glorious golden breastplate soon lay upon his workbench. But Vulcan did not stop there. Taking up his tiny hammer and chisel, he set to work and drew such intricate designs upon the shining objects that Venus could scarcely believe her eyes. Great ships and mighty armies marched across the shield, along with glorious generals and noble statesmen. The sword's hilt looked so much like a snarling wolf's head that the goddess was convinced the eyes were watching her. The red plume of the helmet fanned as though it was already streaming to battle, and the breastplate might have belonged to a god.

Finally, Vulcan laid down his tools and slumped into a chair. "It is finished," he murmured, the light in his eyes dimmed with both fatigue and gentle sadness, "Now the final act of the age of heroes will be worth a song."

Chapter 7: Evander and Pallas

Aeneas and his closest companions had sailed their ship inland, far up the river Tiber. As the sun rose, the first of a group of hills loomed out of the early morning mist, raising the hairs on the back of the prince's neck. It was not fear he felt, but rather a sense of occasion. This place was special, sacred even. "Seven hills," shouted Pandarus from the ship's prow. "Could this be the place the god promised, lord?" Aeneas opened his mouth to reply, but paused, for the morning mist was swirling about him, closing him off from his crew like a wall. The gentle ebb of the river still moved the ship beneath his feet, but all sights and sounds of his friends and the world beyond the mist were gone.

"My son, how far you have come." Aeneas turned to see a beautiful woman with lustrous golden hair standing next to him. He had only seen her a couple of times before in his whole life, but he knew her. Far though they were from the wine-dark sea, the salty crispness of a wave came to his nostrils, mixed with the sweetest of flowers.

"Mother," he barely dared move. "I have only seen you before in my dreams, or when dire need was upon me. What dark tidings do you bring?"

With a smile like the sun, the goddess of love rested a hand upon Aeneas' broad shoulder. "You already know enough of the tidings of war; I bring you a gift of hope." Stepping forwards, she showed her son the miraculous armor made by Vulcan, the smith god. "These are not as powerful as Jupiter's thunderbolt, but they are Vulcan's greatest work. And it is fitting that I give them to you here, where, one day, your children's children shall build the greatest city in the world!"

Lost for words, Aeneas donned the glittering breastplate, strapped on the high-plumed helmet, hung the shining sword from his belt, and slung the glorious shield on his back. Proud tears filled Venus' eyes as she saw her son in his war glory. He could not know it, but with the shield on his back, he was bearing the history of his descendants, for many of their greatest moments had been wrought into the shield's face by the smith god. For a heartbeat, she saw it all: the proud walls with high towers, the temples and the law courts and the markets, the armies of soldiers with rich red cloaks and thick shields marching in perfect unison. Far beyond the horizon's own horizon the mighty city stretched out its hands and found no one to rival it. Then the vision faded, and her son's eager, nervous face was there again.

"Go," she said, wiping her perfect cheeks, "You have already made me so proud, Aeneas, but you have this last task to do: Go and win your destiny."

King Evander had heard about the arrival of the strangers at the court of Latinus. He had heard the rumors that they were Trojans but had scarcely believed them. Tales of the great, decade-long war at Troy had reached Italy some years before and, though he was no mere boy, even Evander's heart lifted at the songs sung of swift-footed Achilles and Hector, tamer of horses. He was not prepared, however, for the arrival of Aeneas. When the hero strode into his hall, everyone present gasped and gaped, for he stood head and shoulders above them all, his armor shining as though he were a god. "The stories barely do justice!" cried Pallas, Evander's eldest son. The young man's eyes shone in Aeneas' reflected glory and his father laid a firm hand on his shoulder before standing to greet their honored guest.

Wine was brought, and all gathered with eager ears as Aeneas told his tale of war and wayward hardship at the hands of the storm, sea, and the fury of the gods. "And so," he concluded, "we have finally reached our destination: Italy has been promised to us as a new home. We do not wish, however, to start our lives here with harsh words and thoughts of invasion. Rather, I would make peace with all, and find ourselves a quiet place far from others where we would not cause any anguish." He sighed, "But Prince Turnus finds fault in us and sees us as a threat. Therefore, I come to you, wise king, and ask for your friendship and your aid. We have no ties of blood or oaths long spoken, yet I beg this of you: will you stand alongside us or at least hold your hand from joining with our foes?"

Pallas dragged his eyes away from the hero's face to stare at his father, waiting to hear his response. Evander noticed his son's look and smiled. The young man was already grown but knew little of war save what the bards sang. The king had fought his fair share and remembered far too much. "Aeneas, son of Anchises, you do us honor by this request. War is a terrible thing, and Turnus is a fool to stoke the fires so rashly. He does not know where the sparks will catch or what they shall destroy unbidden. He is a bully and a thug who thinks too little and acts too swiftly. Such a man makes a bad neighbor. My men shall stand at your side and more," he clapped his hand on his son's shoulder, "I shall send Pallas with you. I shudder to recall the crush of the shield wall, when phalanxes clash and spears pierce, but I can think of no better man to teach him the ways of battle than you, who alone of his race survived the greatest war our world has ever seen."

Thus it was, that Pallas rode at Aeneas' right hand at the head of the Arcadian army. Being miles from the sea, Evander had no ships to lend along with his troops, and yet the stout legs of his men made light of the distance. Within two days, therefore, they had already passed the high walls of Latinum and were nearing the site of the Trojan camp. "When we arrive," remarked Aeneas to Pallas, "I will leave the ordering of your camp to you. War is more than drawing your sword and telling your men to charge. You must arrange your men wisely and ensure for their good care. That is..." but he stopped mid-sentence as they crested the final ridge before the long slope down to the sea and the mooring of the Trojan fleet.

"What's wrong, Prince Aeneas?" asked Pallas. Following the hero's gaze, he saw the shapely prows of the Trojan ships with their tall masts. He saw a sturdy wall of timber and a wide gate enclosing ordered rows of tents. From between the tents rose slender columns of smoke, marking where cooking fires prepared meals for the many hungry mouths. But this was not what had distracted Aeneas. Before the camp, and around it like a terrible, lurking predator, stood a great army, with many banners snapping in the wind off the sea. "The Rutulians!" gasped Pallas, "and the Volsci and the Etruscans! How did Turnus collect such an army so quickly?"

"It does not matter," snapped Aeneas, and Pallas was shocked at his sudden sternness. "What matters is what we do now to rescue my people." Wheeling his horse around, he cried to the army which already was forming up along the ridge. "We close at a run, strike wherever the enemy gathers. We cannot hope to encircle them, so we must divide them, and give my Trojans time to sally forth!" Drawing his sword, he held it aloft and it blazed like a lightning bolt in the sunlight. "Stay by me, Pallas," he instructed. "No matter what, stay by me."

Unfortunately, the Arcadians did not catch the Rutulians' army entirely unaware. Swift scouts had brought word to Turnus of Aeneas' approach, and as he saw the troops amassing behind him, Turnus roared like a bear and led the charge up the slope. The clash of these two armies was like when two storms meet in the mountains. Vast clouds billow up and smash against each other with thunderous tumult. Lighting crashes, rain slams down in torrents, and the rocks beneath crack in terror. So it was as the shield walls collided. Men screamed, swords rang, shields banged, spears splintered. The air was thick with arrows and javelins. The ground was wet with blood. Thrust into the horror of battle, Pallas realized all too quickly that no bard can ever have seen it in real life. It was all too awful. But he was of the blood of Arcas and Lycaon, and he raised his shield and fought with all the skill his father had trained into him his whole life. As Aeneas had instructed, he kept as close as he could to the Trojan hero, trying always to keep sight of the glorious gold of Aeneas' shield, or the plume of his helmet.

But the battle pushed them apart, and soon Pallas was lost in the tangle of dueling fighters. Then he heard his own name being called, and he turned with a smile, expecting to see Aeneas rushing towards him. But his stomach turned in terror as he saw, racing towards him with blazing eyes and a red sword to match his cloak, Turnus. "Pallas, you traitorous dog!" the Rutulian roared. "How can you turn your blades against fellow Italians?"

Pallas tried to reply, but Turnus was already swinging his great sword at his head. A dull thud resounded up his arm as he brought his shield up just in time. Heaving the bigger man away, he tried to counter and shout for Aeneas at the same time. "He has left you!" sneered Turnus, knocking Pallas' blade aside with frightening ease. "Trojans have no honor; they have no guts for fighting. Why do you think they cower behind their walls and leave the battle to you?" Pallas shook his head and lashed out wildly, his blade whispering past Turnus' face as the warrior stepped back a pace before lunging forward with a thrust so swift that Pallas barely saw the sword point as it raced towards him. Pain erupted in his chest, and his sight darkened.

Pallas, son of King Evander of Arcadia, had fallen. Slain by the blade of Turnus, his pale eyes stared lifelessly up at the drifting clouds far overhead. Over him, unseen by all, stepped Mars. The god of war stared around the wide battlefield, his expression torn between bursting pride and overwhelming sadness. He knelt by the young man's body and whispered, "You cannot know it, but your death will turn the tide of this battle, brave son of Arcadia. You fought well, though this was your first and last battle." Rising into the air, he left the clashes and cries far behind him as he returned to Mount Olympus. Jupiter, the king of the gods, had called a council, and it would not do to be late.

CHAPTER 8: THE FINAL BATTLE

"Enough!" shouted Jupiter, slamming his fist upon the arm of his throne. The rush of anger blasted his fellow gods like a blast of wind, and they all turned from their bitter arguments to face him. Venus, goddess of love, and Juno, his queen, had just been screaming in rage at each other, their faces flushed, their fists clenched. Many of the other gods had taken sides, their furious voices shaking the walls of Olympus' gleaming marble palace. "Father," began Venus, her eyes red.

"Husband!" cut in Juno, her brows like thunder.

"Enough!" Jupiter silenced them both once more. "Sit and be silent, all of you. This has gone on long enough. The age of heroes is coming to its close. We had all thought the war at Troy would have been its last great adventure, but Odysseus of Ithaca and Aeneas still have tales to tell. Odysseus shall get home. The Fates have already decided this!" This last remark was aimed at his own brother, Neptune, god of the sea, whose hatred for Odysseus surpassed even Juno's for Aeneas.

"But Aeneas and his people have already reached their destination," continued Jupiter, "Despite your best efforts, dear wife." Now he glowered at Juno, who did not dare to interrupt. "Fate is inexorable, even I can only arbitrate a little. The march of history has been slowed long enough; it is time to let it run its course. Aeneas shall find his city; the manner in which that now occurs is up to Mankind to decide. It is their choice alone. Carthage shall rise and these two cities shall clash. Even my eyes cannot see what shall happen then. But as for the here and now, none of us is to interfere anymore!" Glaring around the circle of assembled gods, he nodded, and the very foundations of Olympus shook with that nod. It was decided. Venus rushed to the window and stared down the long winds to the coast of Italy, where the cries of the gulls could barely be heard over the screams of men and the clash of weapons. There the combined armies of the Volsci and the Etruscans were led by Turnus and his Rutulians. They had surrounded the Trojan camp, but Aeneas, leading the Arcadian army loaned to him by king Evander and prince Pallas, had arrived just in time to break the siege. Pallas, however, had already fallen to Turnus' blade. "He was so young," mourned Venus as her eyes fell on his limp body. "How many mothers must lose their sons before this tide of death ends?"

Aeneas shouted to his men to reform their shield wall, "Overlap your shields and hold together!" They had managed to clear a path to the gate of the Trojan camp. With a creaking of hinges, the gate opened, and out marched the Trojan warriors. The Arcadians, panting and bloodied, allowed them to pass through to the front ranks. "Where is Pallas?" the hero cried aloud. "Where is the prince?"

Pandarus, Aeneas' best scout, pointed a shaking hand through the many dueling warriors to where a bright shield lay, the lion of Arcadia proud in its center. At that moment, when Aeneas saw Pallas' body, something broke within him. "I promised his father I would keep him alive!" his voice was choked, as though something was stuck in his throat. "Come with me!"

Driving a wedge through the battle, Aeneas and his companions retrieved the prince's body and bore it back to the camp, lest some further evil befall it. Until that point, Aeneas had always held back, seeking to wound the Italian soldiers, rather than kill. But now, as he returned to the fray, a fire blazed in his eyes the like of which few had seen before. Pandarus recognized it from the day Troy had fallen, when a madness had seized the hero and he had run recklessly into the fight. Now Aeneas, his shining, god-made armor flashing in the sun, strode forth into the battle with such reckless abandon that the Trojans feared he had lost all will to live. But their fears were needless. With strength hardly to be imagined, Aeneas tore through the ranks of Rutulians, shattered the Volsci line, and left a trail of Etruscan dead like a river leading down to the sea. None could stand against his wrath. His shield was like the sun, blinding any who stood before him, and his sword struck like the very thunderbolt of Jupiter himself.

Seeing their men shaking with fear at the approach of the Trojan warlord, many of Turnus' companions turned to him and cried, "We must retreat! We must regroup with our other allies!" But the Rutulian prince would not be persuaded.

"I started this war to cleanse our fair land of these barbarians. I shall end it here today!" Seizing a spear from one of his friends, Turnus bellowed, "Aeneas! You did not see the foolish boy die, did you? You failed to protect him, just as you failed to protect your own city! Last of a ragged house, you have limped here across the sea only to fall short of greatness. Fight me now and learn what true Italians are made of!"

The burning eyes of the Trojan turned to face him, but Turnus alone of the free peoples of Italy was not afraid. As they charged toward each other, like two bulls, who tore up the ground with their vast hooves as they threw all their strength and weight and sped behind their horns, the soldiers of both armies fell back to allow them room. The wind itself stopped, and the waves grew strangely silent, as though the world itself stopped to witness this final combat. With a great leap, Turnus lunged with his spear, which struck the center of Aeneas' shield with a gong like note that made all within hearing shudder. The Trojan's sword sliced through the air and Turnus only just dodged it. Now they were circling each other, like wolves hungry for the kill, awaiting their time to strike. Turnus jabbed again, drawing the counter and catching it on his own shield. Spinning with the speed of a snake, he threw all his weight behind his attack which pierced empty air. His eyes darted around just in time to see the shining shield slam down and break his spear's shaft clean in two.

Aeneas' heart was thundering against his chest, but his sword hand was quite steady. As Turnus threw down the broken shaft and swept out his own weapon, a stillness seemed to empty his mind and calm his raging blood. The Rutulian hero lunged for him, his teeth bared and his eyes wide. But Aeneas just tapped the blade aside. He avoided the next attack with just a step to the right and bashed Turnus hard in the shoulder with his shield, sending him flying. "Now!" whispered a small voice in his head. "Now!" cried Aeneas, and as his enemy got to his feet, the hero hurled himself at him with a whirlwind of stabs and cuts. Forcing Turnus back and back, he stepped right, feinted left, and then drove his sword, made by Vulcan himself, clean through the Rutulian's shield and into his shoulder.

Turnus crashed to the ground, his face suddenly pale. Aeneas placed a foot on the shield and Turnus cried out one last time and went limp. Pulling his sword from the Rutulian's body, Aeneas said, his voice now trembling with rage once more, "We came here in peace, and you unleashed war. You alone hold the blame for all those who have died here. But I will end this war now." Looking across at the Italian army, he shouted, "Your leader is vanquished. This was his fight, and too many of you have paid the price for his arrogance. Collect your fallen comrades and go home!"

Sheathing his sword, Aeneas stepped away from the body of Turnus, his eyes on the horizon. "So ends a fair day of wrath," he murmured. "I pray that I never have to draw this sword again."

Part II

The Etruscan Kings

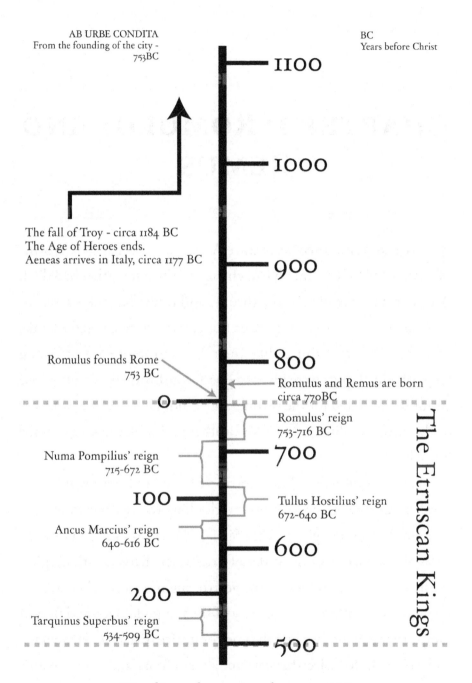

Timeline to be continued at page 118.

Chapter 1: Romulus and Remus

In the three hundred years since Aeneas and his band of Trojans had come to Italy, much had changed. When his father had died, Ascanius had ascended to the throne, and under his rule Lavinium grew so much that a new city, Alba Longa, was founded on the banks of a beautiful lake. But unlike their Trojan forebears, not all the kings of Alba Longa were just and good. The brothers Numitor and Amulius contested for the throne, and although he was the younger of the two, Amulius cast out his brother and took the kingship for himself.

Ashamed in defeat, Numitor took to the hills and would not speak to anyone, living in a cave overlooking the city which was his by right. But his daughter, Rhea Silvia, still served in Alba Longa as a Vestal Virgin, one of the order of priestesses charged with keeping the flame of Vesta, goddess of the hearth, alight. Angry at her father's plight, Rhea went to the sanctuary of the war god, Mars, and prayed long into the night, begging the god for justice. Exhausted from rage and worry, she fell asleep beneath the altar of Mars, and in her dreams she saw the god himself standing before her.

"Daughter of Aeneas' line, I hear your plea," said Mars. "Let your rage be still, for your sons shall bring you the vengeance you seek. This and more: from them shall come the greatest city in Italy and, indeed, the world."

But Rhea Silvia, confused, dared to ask the god another question: "But how? I am of the order of Vesta, sworn never to marry nor bear children."

Mars smiled down on her, "It has already been foretold." Suddenly, he drew his sword and rushed at her.

Rhea woke with a start, her skin coated with cold sweat, and found that it was morning. Somewhere above her, a woodpecker was tapping at a tree. The young priestess drew her cloak tight around her and left the sanctuary, hardly daring to believe what she had dreamed.

Rhea Silvia might not have believed it at first, but in time she realized that she was indeed pregnant. When the time came for her to give birth, she tried to flee the city, only to be caught by Amulius' guards. Dragged before her uncle the king, Rhea stood tall and proud, her hand resting on her swollen belly.

"You have forfeited your vows to the goddess!" Amulius cried, pointing an accusing finger at his niece. "You may be of my blood, but I cannot protect you from this. The child shall be taken from here and abandoned to die. And you shall be cast out, never again to have the protection of our walls and our laws."

"With such a weak, unjust king as you, uncle", Rhea replied, "no citizen is protected by the law nor the walls!"

But her words were empty, for none would disobey the king in his own hall. Soon enough, Rhea gave birth not to one boy, but two.

Amulius did not spare a thought, however, for the mother's tears. He knew that more children on Numitor's side of the family would be a threat to him. But he did not smile as he ordered his men to drag his grieving niece from the city, nor as he sent his most loyal soldier out into the wilderness, the newborn twins tied to his saddle. Thus it was, that as the day drew to a close on the banks of the Tiber, the captain of the royal guard remounted his horse and glanced over his shoulder at where the two tiny babies lay in the grass, wrapped in a single blanket he had not had the heart to remove. It was the worst command he had ever been required to follow. "But at least I did not have to kill them myself," he told himself as he rode home, "the wolves shall do the job for me."

But there the captain was quite wrong. High up on one of the many hills overlooking the river, there was a cave. It was the home of a small wolf pack and that night most of the adults were out hunting. A single female remained behind to keep an eye on the cubs. But the cubs were asleep, and the female was restless. The night breeze brought the cries and the scent of the two young humans to her, but some sense other than sound or smell told her that she must investigate. It was as though the heart in her shaggy chest stirred, like a bird's tiny wingbeats against her ribcage.

Silent and shadowlike, she slipped from the lair and followed her keen sense down to where the wet sounds of the river were cut clean through by the plaintive cries of the tiny humans. But the she-wolf was cautious and suspected a trap. Thus, she remained in the long grass and cast around with ear and eye, sniffing the wind for any foreign scent. But her heart was now throbbing and besides, what creature would use its own young as bait, even for a wolf? So, she padded forward and found the two human-cubs. They were strange creatures, with tiny limbs and only scraps of dark fur on their heads. But their lungs were powerful, for all their size, and the she-wolf flattened her ears to her head against the noise.

She should just kill them and have a welcome snack ready for the hunters when they returned. But as the thought passed through her mind, her heart shook within her chest and she began to pant as though with sudden terror. Flopping down besides the two helpless, bald cubs, the she-wolf felt the throbbing subside. One of the human-cubs' tiny hands flailed and stroked her muzzle, sending a thrill up through her hackles down to the tip of her tail. But it was not fear nor pain that smote her in the darkness. Rather, it was that wonderful feeling when a pack-sister had given birth to a litter and the whole pack gathered around to greet the new cubs with gentle licks and nuzzling. Certainty blossomed in her mind like the sun dawning on a new day. The human-cubs were wrapped in some strange, soft woolen stuff, and the she-wolf used this now to slowly drag them up the slope to the den. Something about the movement silenced the two little creatures. Once they were quietly snuggled up to the still-sleeping wolf-cubs, the she-wolf offered them her milk. The two boys drank greedily and then fell asleep, tiny hands looped in the thick fur of the wolf-cubs.

As the new day dawned, the rest of the pack returned. The strange sent of the two newcomers to their den made them wary, but surprise replaced fear when their bright eyes fell on the twins. The she-wolf was exhausted, for they had woken many times in the night and were constantly hungry. But as the two lead wolves approached the defenseless scraps of life, she growled a warning as though they were her own blood. A soft nose touched one of the boys' heads and the lead wolf leaped back as though stung. Joy soared in the she-wolf's heart, for she knew that her pack-brother had felt it too: that strange pull in the heart. None of the pack would harm her two human-cubs, of that she was certain.

Outside the den, invisible to all, even the keen-eyed wolves, Mars sat and smiled as the dawn's red light sparkled on the waters of the river Tiber. His sons were now safe and would grow strong on the she-wolf's milk. In time he would arrange for some shepherd to find them, for although wolves were his favorite animals, they must be raised among humans. Rising to his feet, he lifted his spear and was gone from the hillside in a flash.

Chapter 2: The Palatine and the Aventine

M any years had passed since the she-wolf had taken in two scrawny newborn humans. Mars had not been idle, and as the boys had turned one year old he caused a sheep from the flock of Faustulus, a kindly man, to get lost on the very hill where the wolf-den lay. In search of the lost ewe, the shepherd had heard the babies' laughter and rushed to find them. The ewe lay dead, and the she-wolf, blood still dripping from her jaws, watched as Faustulus skidded to a halt, his eyes wide with terror. But when the great grey beast did not leap at his throat, the shepherd found his courage and crept inside the low cave. There he found the young boys and, taking them in his arms, he left the hill. The she-wolf watched him go; her task was complete.

Romulus and Remus had thus grown up under the care of Faustulus, their names coming to the shepherd in a dream. He was a simple man, but not foolish; he guessed that these two boys might be the children of the Vestal Virgin who had been cast of Alba Longa the previous year. The fact that he dreamed their names only raised his suspicions. But he did not waver in his first instinct to care for the twins as though they were his own sons. He and his wife had no children, and thus Romulus and Remus brought a joy into their lives which they had never thought possible.

Perhaps it was the wolf-milk on which they had been raised, or perhaps it was the fresh water and sweet fruits of the Tiber valley, but the two boys grew strong and tall. They ran up and down the seven hills around which Faustulus and the other herdsmen grazed their flocks and soon were known widely not only for their physical prowess, but also for their fairness and quick thinking.

There came a day, however, when the twins were strong young men. Tax collectors in the service of King Amulius came, as they did every year, and demanded the tithe that was owed the king. Many, however, thought that the taxmen were lining their own pockets as well as those of their master. Remus was there, but Romulus was away on the Aventine with the flock. And when Remus stood up to argue with the servants of the king, harsh words followed. One of the men went to strike this tall, rude young man, but Remus fought back and was arrested by the guards.

Romulus came home that evening to find his parents in tears. Hearing the news, he decided immediately to rescue his brother. "He would not hesitate to do the same for me," he said and, taking his spear with which he guarded the flocks, set about calling together as many men as he could. To his surprise, dozens answered the call, for the taxmen had been cheating the poor folk for many years and anger flowed through the hills as strong and as fast as the Tiber. By chance, word of this rebellion against Amulius came to the ears of Numitor and Rhea Silvia, who had joined her father in his hillside exile. Something in their hearts told them that they should go and see this brave young man and, hurrying as fast as the old man's legs would allow, they came to the Palatine hill.

Romulus stood there among the crowd of herdsmen, farmers, and simple merchants. "My friends, for too long have we been silent while the greedy thieves who claim to serve our king steal the food from our tables. Our king, I say, but I never swore allegiance to him. By what right does he rule these lands? None! We shall take back my brother from Amulius and, in doing so, show that false king that there is freedom and justice in the lands of the Tiber!"

A chill ran down Numitor's spine. He was wise and sensed that the Fates were stretching out the threads of their endless tapestry. Looking at his daughter, and then back at Romulus, he saw the similarities between them. "Romulus!" his old voice shook as he strode forward, a thick stick supporting his faltering feet. "You do not know how much truth you speak. I am Numitor, elder brother to Amulius and the rightful king of Alba Longa. More than this: I am your grandfather." For the first time, perhaps ever, Romulus was lost for words. Then Rhea Silvia rushed forward to stand by her father, tears in her eyes, and he knew that they did not lie. The three embraced, and there was not a man there who was not moved by this sudden, unlooked-for reunion.

"Come friends!" called Romulus, "Come and let us take back what is ours!"

Night was falling over Alba Longa and the guards were sleepy at their posts. The night was cold, and those few who weren't hunched around log fires were standing huddled in their cloaks, barely sparing a thought for what might be coming from the hills. As a result, none saw Romulus climb over the wall and let down a rope. None heard the brigade of invaders, armed with spears and pitchforks, as they snuck along the quiet streets. Numitor led them, for although he was old, he knew the streets better than any of them, though it was twenty years since he had last trod their wide paving stones. Only one of Amulius' men looked up when they entered the prison and he was silenced by a swift thrust of Romulus' spear. "Brother," whispered Remus from his cell, "it took you long enough!" Romulus laughed and within moments Remus, the guard's sword in hand, was free. But they did not turn to leave. "We have come this far. Why not right the wrong which caused our family to be torn asunder?" said Romulus. "Let us cast out this tyrant Amulius and set our grandfather back on his throne." All agreed, and so Numitor, his eyes bright, guided them deeper into his old city.

As Remus and Romulus burst into the palace itself, Amulius just stood there in shock as his brother, whom he had thought long dead, strode up the hall, while the twins and their men easily overcame the handful of guards. "What are you going to do to me?" The king cried as Romulus leveled his spear at him and Remus felt the edge of his sword. "Do you not know that to spill the blood of your kin is the worst crime of all? The gods shall punish you if you do not let me live!"

"Your crimes, great-uncle," said Remus, "against your own family have gone unanswered for too long. You cast out the rightful king, you cast out your own niece, and you would have seen my brother and I die on the banks of the Tiber. You did not even have the courage to do the deed yourself." He glanced at Romulus, who nodded. "That is where we are different!" With one motion, both twins struck, striking down the king and sending his crown rolling across the floor.

"The tyrant is dead!" called Romulus, picking up the crown and gesturing to Numitor to sit on the throne.

"Long live King Numitor!" cried Remus, and the cheers woke all the people of Alba Longa, few of whom shed a tear for Amulius, who had been as cruel to them as he had to those beyond the walls.

Although Numitor and their mother begged them to stay, Romulus and Remus desired greatly to build their own city, as they had promised the men who had followed them to Alba Longa. Thus it was that they returned to the seven hills where they had grown up. But for the first time in their lives, the twins came into conflict. Romulus wanted to build the city on the Palatine hill, for it was the tallest and most central. Remus preferred the Aventine, for while it was shorter, it was wider and offered far more space on which to build. The argument burned between these two, whom all had thought inseparable. Finally, they agreed to ask the gods for a sign. Each went to the summit of their preferred hill and offered sacrifices to the gods. Then they waited. A cry went up from the Aventine hill, as Remus pointed to a group of six vultures flocking overhead. Moments later, Romulus too raised his hand and thanked the gods with joy, for twelve vultures had flapped above the Palatine.

However, this did not solve their rivalry, for Remus claimed that his sign had come first, and therefore the gods favored his choice. But Romulus pointed out that only six vultures had come to the

Aventine, while twelve had shown themselves over the Palatine. And so, they parted, the wrath of each as hot as the other's. Remus began building walls around the summit of his hill, and Romulus did the same on his.

There came a day when Romulus' walls had reached waist height, and he heard the familiar voice of Remus as his brother ascended the hill. Despite their argument, Romulus was glad to see his twin, and waved at him as he came closer. "Have you come to admit that my hill is better at last?" he asked, half-mockingly. "I can see from here that my walls are already higher!"

A nasty look came over Remus' face. "Your walls?" he sneered, "They couldn't keep a sheep out." With a sudden burst of speed, he leaped clean over the wall and landed near to his brother. "Do you see?" he shouted, turning to leap again. But rage, the like of which he had never known, blazed in Romulus' chest. Hefting a great stone in his hands, he hurled it at Remus. His brother fell and did not rise again.

Many of Romulus' men stared, aghast, but Romulus leaped up onto the wall and shouted, "None shall dare cross our walls again. This is Rome, and it shall rule the world!"

CHAPTER 3: THE SABINE WOMEN

Although the murder of Remus cast a dark cloud over the valley between the hills, none dared challenge Romulus for the kingship. Thus it was that Rome came into being. Romulus built his own home on the Palatine hill, and many of his closest friends and followers did likewise. In the fertile valley of the River Tiber, wide fields were plowed and sown. Men cut back the forests and built sturdy houses. Thus far, Romulus' dreams were coming true, except for one thing: There were few women and fewer children. Many men had flocked to follow him, and it was their strong arms which protected the herds, guided the plows, and built the walls. But only a handful of them were married.

Romulus knew that, if he did not solve this simple but vital problem, then Rome would be a ghost town within a generation. Thus it was that he concocted a plan, and sent out messengers to several nearby tribes, including the Sabines. "King Romulus of Rome invites you all to games in honor of Neptune, the sea god!" they proclaimed. "There shall be wine and food for all, and prizes for the glorious athletes. We ask only one thing: respect the hospitality of the divine Neptune and King Romulus by leaving your weapons at home."

The chieftains of the tribes were surprised but gladdened by this sudden peaceful gesture from Romulus, and many accepted gladly, bringing their fastest and strongest men, as well as their families. The Roman king presided over the games with a broad smile, a great red cloak about his shoulders. The prizes he awarded were fine indeed: golden wreaths and great jars of wine, or silver belts and bejeweled swords. Even Titus Tatius, king of the Sabines, was forced to admit that the Romans had achieved much in their short time and said as much to Romulus, "If this is what your people can achieve in a few short years, I wonder what you shall do in a hundred!" Romulus smiled and offered his guest another cup of wine.

All the Sabines and the other tribes were drinking and eating heartily, but the Roman men did not touch a drop of wine. When asked about this, they all answered, "Our priests have forbidden us from drinking on this night sacred to Neptune, but that is a law only for Romans. Please, enjoy the fruits of our vineyards!" As night fell, torches were lit, and Romulus stood upon a table to cheers and much stamping. He held up a hand for silence, and looked around at all present, noticing with satisfaction that the eyes of his guests were hazy with wine. "Romans!" he called, "it is time!" And he took off his cloak, folded it and then laid it on his shoulder.

This was the signal the Romans had been waiting for. Swords appeared from beneath their own cloaks, and they grabbed at the young women the Sabines and the other tribes had brought with them. The men tried to fight back, but they stumbled and fell and were driven back by the bright blades, red in the firelight. Half of Romulus' forces drove the men off, while the other half carried the screaming and crying women away. They had taken only the unmarried women and young girls who would grow to become strong mothers. Romulus himself seized a beautiful woman with dark eyes called Hersilia, and he carried her away to his home, not letting her feet touch the floor until she was in his own house. Aside from the violence done to drive off the drunken men, no harm befell the Sabine women, for Romulus' orders had been very clear: "We must use violence to take them, but violence will never keep them, nor make them our own wives."

The heads of the Sabines were heavy the next day, and their hearts were full of anger. Titus Tatius roared with fury, but none of his men were in any state to fight back that day. "And besides, my lord," said one of his wise advisors, "Even with every man ready and armed, we cannot hope to match the Romans in combat. They may have few women, but every man of theirs is equal to two of ours. And do not forget their walls atop the high hills: A hundred men could defend those heights from a thousand."

Thus, Titus Tatius had to bide his time, and he went to the other tribes to persuade them to join with him in the war against Romulus.

Meanwhile, back in Rome, the Sabine women were surprised at the courtesy and kindness with which the Romans treated them. As time went on, most came to enjoy the well-built homes and lush valleys between the Palatine, the Aventine, and the Capitoline hills. Many, indeed, took husbands and, in time, bore children. Even Hersilia, who had at first scratched and screamed at Romulus, saw, after a while, that he was a good man and a fine king. Thus it was that Rome gained its first queen. But Titus Tatius wanted his daughter back, and eventually he managed to persuade his fellow chieftains to join him. Together they marched on Rome.

As the two armies lined up, a young prince, Caenina, spurred his horse up to Titus. "Lord king!" he cried, "Our armies are ready, but let us not make all these men die needlessly. I shall challenge Romulus to single combat, just as Hector and Achilles of old. If he is as brave as the Romans say he is, he shall not refuse, and we shall get our women back without great slaughter." Titus paused for a moment, but the young man spoke sense.

Riding out into the middle of the open space between the armies, Caenina shouted his challenge, hurling a spear toward the Roman ranks. Such was his skill, that the blade struck the ground within a stride of the front rank. Romulus dismounted and strode to meet his challenger.

A roar went up from both armies as the two men drew their swords and charged. Caenina was younger and faster than Romulus, but the Roman king was taller and stronger, and he had grown up in this valley. He knew every inch of it, every stone, every tuft of grass. Thus it was that he drove the young warrior back and, choosing his moment, he lunged. Caenina caught the blade in the middle of his shield, but the force of Romulus' lunge sent him flying backward over a tree root. His own weapon went flying and he could only yell with terror as the king brought his sword down upon him.

The Roman cheers of triumph echoed from hill to hill, and Romulus raised his sword, gesturing to his men to follow him, "Come Romans! They are here to drive us from our land. Let us now show them what Romans are truly made of!"

Titus Tatius, never a coward, did not falter. "For our women, our families, and our honor!" he roared.

But then an incredible thing came to pass: As the Sabines and the Romans marched forward, a third army entered the battlefield. This army, however, bore no shields, wore no armor, and carried no weapons. The Roman wives, the stolen Sabine women, were rushing into the space between the advancing forces. Silent, but no less fierce than the men, they formed a line between the Romans and the Sabines, facing both. Their hair was long, their faces set, and in their arms they held their newborn children.

Out from the center of the women's line stepped Hersilia, and even Romulus did not dare approach her, such was the fury upon her face. "Is this what you want?" She cried, and every man heard her words for silence had fallen like a spell. "If you would take up swords against each other, then you must cut through us to do so. We are your daughters and your wives. We are the mothers of your children and your grandchildren. The Romans may have taken us, but we chose to stay. So let blood be spilled, but if we are the reason you fight, then we shall be the first to die!"

A ringing silence followed her words, and then a sudden movement came from both armies. Soldiers ran out from both sides, but they were flinging away their weapons, tossing aside their shields. Sabine fathers ran to their daughters, Roman husbands hugged their wives, and where moments before two armies had stood, there now could be seen only a myriad families. Children squeaked with laughter and happy tears flowed, for all thoughts of battle had been forgotten. Somehow, Romulus managed to push his way through to Hersilia, and held her closely to him. "What a queen I have married," he gasped, staring into her eyes.

She smiled back at him, "You said it yourself, dear husband: violence will never turn a woman into a wife. It takes more than a bright sword to build a kingdom."

CHAPTER 4: NUMA AND ANCUS

After thirty-seven glorious years on the throne, Romulus finally died. Some said that he had been taken by the gods up to heaven as a rightful son of Mars. Regardless, Rome faced a problem, for Romulus had died without a son to take on the throne. Romulus had left behind him a council called the Senate, which was made up of the heads of the most important families in the city. It was they, therefore, that took on full responsibility for governing the city and its surrounding land. For five days in turn, one of the senators would sit on Romulus' throne and chair the meetings of the Senate. This "interrex" chose who should speak next and organized the votes for the various decisions that had to be made.

This comfortable solution did not last long, however. Swiftly two factions arose: the Romans and the Sabines, remnants of the original tribes who had been brought together by Romulus. Rome was on the brink of civil war, and the Senate desperately searched for a compromise candidate to fill the throne, for they now understood that while they were wise and capable, the senators needed one to stand above them all and rule with authority. Beyond Rome's borders, the neighboring tribes were becoming restless and hostile, seeing the lack of a Roman ruler as a sign of weakness and a chance to grab back land which Romulus had secured during his reign. Casting around from among their number, it was clear that none of the senators would be accepted by either faction. There was too much politics, too many long-standing rivalries. They needed an outsider, but still one who could unite them.

"I know a man," said Vibius Tatius, the son of Titus, leader of the Sabine faction, "a man who none of you can deny will rule well." Sneering smiles and jeers were the main response to his announcement, but the interrex called for order and Vibius was allowed to continue. "Not far from where we stand lies the small town of Cures," he explained. "There lives a friend of mine and of many here, Roman and Sabine. A man learned in the laws, both written by the gods and by men. He is noble and wise, resolute and firm. His name is Numa Pompilius." There was an instant uproar from the Roman senators.

"He's a Sabine!" they crowed, "No surprise there. You want a Sabine puppet who you can control."

Again the interrex called for order, and Tatius stepped forward, addressing Marcus, the head of the Roman faction individually.

"Do you know Numa?" he asked, and Marcus nodded.

"Is he a good man?" Reluctantly, Marcus agreed.

"Is he smarter than me? Is he smarter than you?" Marcus paused for a moment, but he was, in his heart, an honest man. "He is," he replied.

Returning to the center of the room, Vibius Tatius raised his voice to address the now silent senators. "Brothers, Roman or Sabine, I see no difference. I do not ask for the crown, nor do I recommend Numa for any other reason than the ones your Marcus has agreed to: He is a good and clever man. We have many warriors in Rome, but little justice. Let us ask the best to lead us, regardless of their bloodline." Silently, the senators raised their hands, as they would to vote. Many of them. More than half! Vibius smiled. "I shall go to him today, if you, Marcus will come with me?"

Numa lived in a small villa in the center of Cures. Unlike the senators, whose cloaks were edged with an expensive purple fabric, his tunic was no different from that of his slaves, simple, clean, and practical. A frown creased the older man's brows as he welcomed Vibius and Marcus into his study, where hundreds of scrolls were piled neatly on shelves. Having accepted wine, the two senators explained the reason for their visit: to offer Numa the crown.

For a few moments Numa sat in silent astonishment, then he shook his head. "No. How can I be king? Rome is a country at war, and I am a man of peace."

Marcus and Vibius glanced at each other.

"That is why it must be you!" exclaimed Marcus. "Rome needs to prove to the world that it is more than a city of soldiers. We must show that the best men among us can also reason and pray and judge. You can do those things."

Numa bowed his head in solemn thought. Then he rose and headed out into his garden, his eyes on the floor. Standing under a tree, still staring resolutely at the ground, he said, "Romulus was son of Mars himself, they say. I cannot claim such divinity, but if the gods will it that I take on this great duty, then they shall send a sign. Raising his eyes to the sky, he looked long and hard, Marcus and Vibius following his line of sight. A terrified gasp escaped the older man as a great eagle dove into view at that moment, flying from his right in the direction of Rome. The two men held their breath as Numa turned back to them, his face set. "Jupiter himself has sent me this sign," he told them gravely, "Let it be so. I shall rule Rome."

Since the days of Romulus, the mighty first king of the city he had founded and named after himself, over 180 years had passed. After Numa, his nephew Tullus Hostilius was elected as king by the senators. But while Numa had sought to govern with a gentle, guiding hand, Tullus had ruled with an iron fist. He had carved out more land for the new city-state from its neighbors, making few friends and many enemies. Rome might still be a small state amid the wide, fertile lands of central Italy, but no-one doubted the strength of its soldiers or the ferocity of its ruler.

When Tullus' daughter married the grandson of Numa, however, a new word entered the Roman language: dynasty. Like it or not, there was no-one who could challenge young Ancus Marcius for the crown when Tullus finally died, and so the next in this line of kings took the throne. But sullen muttering could be heard throughout the courtyards and colonnades of Rome. The people, young and old, rich and poor, were not happy with this automatic succession. It did not help matters that, unlike his father-in-law, Ancus did not fit the image of a strong, warrior-king. Shorter than most, his left arm was strangely bent, which had always meant that he had difficulty holding a shield. Some went so far as to see this as a bad sign, for how could a man who struggled to defend himself in combat hope to defend those he ruled?

It was then that Ancus surprised them. When the Latins, the tribe who had lived in Italy since before Aeneas himself had come to those shores, began to claim back land that Tullus had taken from them, Ancus sent ambassadors, not soldiers, to solve the problem. Many seized this opportunity to publicly question their new ruler. Even in the senate, where Ancus sat in the throne of Romulus, there was dissent and debate. "A king should be strong!" cried some of the senators, "He should not shrink from a fight. Who else will protect our people? The Latins can smell weakness!"

Ancus turned to them with a slow, deliberate look on his face. In a low voice that reverberated throughout the hallowed hall, he replied, "It is not a strength simply to lash out, but a lack of control. It is not a weakness to extend a hand and seek a common solution, but rather maturity. Since our people came to these shores, we have fought and stolen, pillaged and burned. But citizens cannot live like bandits. We are the children of Romulus, descended from the mighty Aeneas himself. The gods themselves are our ancestors! We must be better than mere mortals, scavenging like dogs for scraps of meat."

It did not surprise anyone that Ancus' ambassadors returned with nothing but a scornful reply from the Latins. All eyes in the Senate turned to their young king, who rose, that same deliberate expression adorning his face. "It is time to open the temple of Janus, my friends," was all he said. The next day, the horns were blown in the Field of Mars, the wide space beyond the city's walls where, it was said, Aeneas had done battle with Turnus, all those years ago. Farmers who normally goaded their oxen forward left their fields; merchants closed their shops; and ships were left at the harbor. Swords were sharpened, spears were readied, and shields were hefted onto strong arms. With King Ancus at its head, the army of Rome marched forth, and within days the fields of the Latins ran red with blood. Victory followed victory, and within a month, Ancus had secured not just the land his father-in-law had once taken, but such was his nobility and grace in victory, that many of the Latins left the rule of their own chieftains and begged to join Rome as citizens.

On his return, the oldest and most venerable of the senators bowed in awe and gratitude to their young king. One stepped forward and addressed their victorious ruler with new reverence, "Sire, before we doubted you, but that has now passed. Forgive us and tell us how you achieved such triumph."

Ancus Marcius looked down from his throne at the wise old man and smiled, "I did what my father-in-law forgot to do, senator: I fought a just war. Victory for the sake of victory is not worthy of our city. Victory in defense of what is ours, that furthers our cause and brings us glory and riches and new allies, that I call "just". We extended the hand of friendship and when that was met with scorn, only then did we respond with the fist of war. If we do so always, always shall we be victorious."

CHAPTER 5: THE FALL OF THE LAST KING

In the 209th year since Romulus' founding of the city, Rome's seventh king took the throne. I say "took" for it is doubtful that his predecessor, Servius Tullius, died of natural causes. Some say he was poisoned, some that he was strangled in his sleep. All that is known for certain is that Lucius Tarquinus Superbus became king to the surprise and horror of many, for he was a violent man. It was sadly appropriate that his last name meant "arrogant", and he was subsequently always known as Tarquin the Proud, but not to his face.

Early in his reign, there came to Rome a wise woman, the Sibyl of Cumae. She was descended from the same Sibyl who had guided Aeneas through the Underworld, back when the Age of Heroes was just ending. Apollo, the great god of prophecy, spoke through her, and she had written down the future of Rome on nine great scrolls. Standing at the gates of the city, the Sibyl demanded an audience with King Tarquin, but would not enter the city, for her position as priestess of Apollo meant she should remain apart from people as much as possible.

On hearing the news, Tarquin refused to leave his palace. "I am king of Rome, descended from Romulus himself!" he said, "If this fortune-teller wishes to petition me, she can do so like the rest of the rabble."

Days later, when Tarquin happened to be leaving the city to go hunting, the Sibyl was there again, and this time Tarquin consented to speak to her. Eying her simple tent and meager campfire, Tarquin told her to be quick.

"Behold, great king, the future of Rome!" cried the Sibyl, and laid the scrolls out before him.

"Old crones like you never want something for nothing," scoffed Tarquin. "How much for your wondrous prophecies?"

"Nine scrolls, nine talents of gold," replied the old woman, her gaze never wandering from the king.

"You're mad!" Tarquin shouted. "You should be lucky if I don't have you whipped!"

Without a word, the Sibyl picked up three of the heavy scrolls and tossed them on the fire. Turing back to the king she said, "Six scrolls, nine talents of gold."

Tarquin's face went red, but his eyes darted first to the remaining six scrolls, and then to the campfire, where the last scraps of parchment were collapsing into ash.

"With nine talents I could build five, even six warships, old woman!" he growled. "Lower your price, and I'll consider it."

The Sibyl did not hesitate. Sweeping three more scrolls into her arms, she dumped on top of the flames. Tarquin made a desperate grab for them, but he was too late. The fire consumed the dry parchment with a crackle and a snap.

"Three scrolls, nine talents of gold," said the old woman, her eyes sparkling with amusement as Tarquin ground his teeth and clenched his fists. "Fine!" he shouted, and called to his servants to have the heavy gold bars brought from his treasury. "These had better be worth it, you wrinkled old crone!" he hissed as the talents were exchanged for the three remaining scrolls.

The Sibyl shrugged, "If one has the wisdom to read and understand the scrolls, Rome will prosper." She looked hard at the king, who was holding the three rolls of parchment like they were his firstborn children. "It remains to be seen if you have such a mind."

But it seemed that Tarquin the Proud was not the wise man he thought he was. Not only could he not understand the scrolls, for they referenced times and events he could not recognize, but his shortcomings did not stop at the un-fogging of the future. Desiring to make his mark on the city, Tarquin decided to build more seats for the great Circus, the chariot racetrack. But the cost ended up being twice what he had originally planned. Blaming his architects, the proud king turned his eye on the Tarpeian Rock, which overlooked the Forum. Deciding that it would serve as a good lookout point, he had the top of the rock leveled. Too late, it became clear that the Tarpeian Rock was too central to see far beyond the seven hills of Rome. Indeed, the only good idea Tarquin had was to dig a great trench through the middle of the city to act as a sewer, where all the waste could be dumped and washed away by three streams which he had diverted for the purpose. But the streams did not seem to like their new channels, and flooded the streets of Rome on a regular basis.

All these projects cost money, and so Tarquin decided to rebuild both his treasury and his standing in the eyes of the people by first raiding and then openly declaring war on his neighbors: The Rutulii, descendants of Turnus, the foe of Aeneas. If Tarquin excelled anywhere, it was in battle. But the Rutulii were a rich people with a great army, and his ill-advised war took far longer than anyone would have expected or hoped.

Lucius Junius Brutus, a member of the Senate, who was supposed to advise the king but whom Tarquin frequently ignored, decided one day that enough was enough. As the Senate gathered, Brutus raised his voice and said, "Fellow Senators, the time has come to face the truth." Pointing at the empty throne, he continued, "Tarquin the Proud is not here. When was the last time any of us can remember him taking part in our meetings? He rules, but without wisdom or foresight. We could help him, as this hallowed chamber has always done, but he ignores us. Worse: he refuses to appoint new senators when those of us who have grown old and weary in service to Rome finally succumb to time's arrow. Any authority we have is steadily crumbling. We must act or Rome will collapse from within!"

"But what can we do?" cried some of the senators. "He is the king, descended from Romulus, or so he claims. And who would stand in his stead? You, Brutus? By what right?"

Striding up onto the raised platform of the king, Brutus kicked the throne and sent it crashing to the floor. "I do not want to be king! Let the best men of the Senate, the two consuls, lead us. They are elected each year, and with two at the top, no one man can ever control all of Rome. But you are right: to depose a king is a great and terrible act. As wise and as solemn as this body of men is, we alone cannot make this decision. Call together the assembly of the people. We shall speak to them and convince them of this course."

And so it was that Tarquin was brought to the Field of Mars by the senators, and there he stood aghast as the people of Rome assembled. Such a thing had not been seen in the 25 years he had sat on the throne. "I've been crowned once before," he quipped, trying to sound braver than he felt, "Why do it a second time?"

But the stony faces of the senators quietened him. Brutus stepped forth once more and, in a ringing voice, spoke to the people of Tarquin's reign. "Finally," he roared, pointing an accusatory hand at the king, "Do you want such a man to continue to rule? I say to you today, Tarquin the Proud is no rightful king. He is nothing but a tyrant, a fool, a scavenger of gold. If Romulus were here today, he would not turn away in disgust, he would hurl himself from the Tarpeian Rock! Speak, Romans, let the gods know your choice. Should Tarquin the Proud rule?"

"No!" the blast of the combined voice of the Roman citizens threatened to deafen the king as his sentence tolled like a great bell. His shoulders slumped, his legs shook, and for the first time in his life, Tarquin did not know what to say. Removing the circlet of gold from his forehead, he tossed it on the floor. Then, without a word, without raising his eyes from the ground, the last king of Rome shuffled from the stage.

Part III

Hannibal-Rome's Worst Nightmare

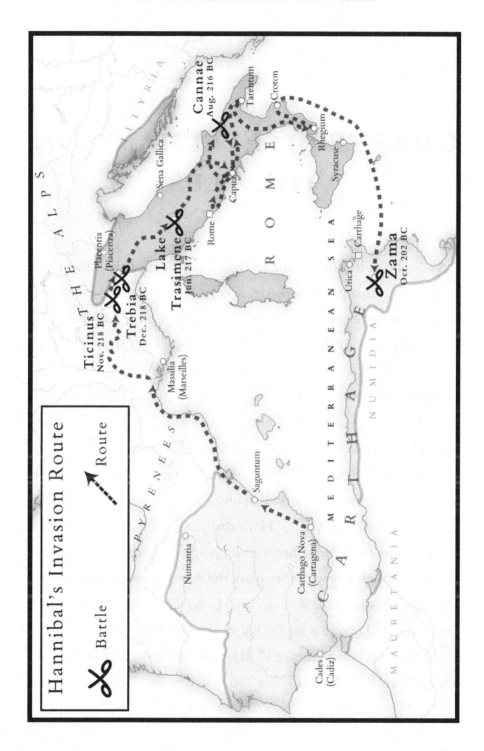

CHAPTER 1: ELEPHANTS IN THE ALPS

As the columns of smoke rose from Saguntum, crows and vultures began their eerie descent. The town had fallen that morning in a crescendo of screams and scrapes of iron on iron. But the victorious army did not rush through the streets, stealing all they could find, for their general, a tall, dark man with hawk-like eyes, had forbidden it. "The people of Saguntum are not to blame for their leaders' folly," he said, "They chose to side with Rome, and see how Rome has left them, defenseless against our warriors."

"Brother," Hasdrubal, the cavalry commander, "Rome will not stand idly by while we attack their allies."

"They started this war," Hannibal cut across him. "Saguntum lies south of the River Ebro, the long agreed border between our provinces. By allying with this town, the Romans sought only to gain a foothold in our land. Why do you think? To invade. But an attack that is stopped before it begins harms the aggressor far more."

"What are you planning?" Mago, Hannibal and Hasdrubal's younger brother asked, "I know you swore to father that you would always be Rome's enemy, but even he wouldn't poke the wolf like you are doing. The Adirim will not support this line of action."

"They will have no choice!" hissed the general, his eyes flashing. "Rome will counter-attack, and when they do, we shall already have invaded their lands."

"How?" cried the two brothers together. But Hannibal would only smile and turn his eyes away to the north.

Hasdrubal was right: No sooner had news reached the floor of the Roman Senate than they sent a delegation led by Quintus Fabius Maximus. One of the greatest statesmen of the Roman Republic, Fabius had already twice been elected consul, the most senior magistracy in Rome. With a beak-like nose and piercing eyes, few of the Adirim would maintain eye-contact with him as he strode into their hall.

"I will be brief," he snapped, slicing through the usual hubbub. "Saguntum remains an ally of Rome. The army which sacked it shall be disbanded and the general, this Hannibal Barca, shall be handed over to face Roman justice. I need not remind you that it is scarcely twenty-five years since the end of the last war between our two peoples, and you all remember how that went! In the 535 years that Rome has stood, it has never been defeated." Then he gripped his toga in both hands, "I hold in my toga peace," he gestured with one hand, "and war," he gestured with the other hand. "Which will you choose?"

One of the two Sufetes, who led the Adirim, stepped forward. "Carthage stood long before Rome, Fabius Maximus. You come into our hall with your proud words and your vile threats. Such arrogance demands that you choose. What will Rome decide?"

Fabius did not hesitate. With a jerk, he raised his fist high in the air and bellowed, "War!"

Fabius had not been lying. For twenty years, Carthage and Rome had fought a bitter war across the Mediterranean. The Romans had begun it by invading the island of Sicily, which Carthage had owned for centuries. But by the end, Carthage's once proud navy was nothing more than rotting hulks on the sea floor, and Rome had become masters of the seas. They had not, however, been able to crush the vast armies and the wide-ranging empire which Carthage had built, and so these two great powers had glared at each other across the waves. Fabius, therefore, had rushed back to Italy to prepare Rome's legions, amassing them on the southern part of the peninsula as well as the island of Sicily itself. "They will want to regain their old territory, at the very least," he told his fellow senators. "With its rich farmland, Sicily is a fertile jewel."

But they had forgotten Hannibal. Far to the west, on the coast of Iberia, the general stared out over the sea to where, he knew, lay the mouth of the great river Tiber. "It is time to march," he said, turning back to his brothers.

"March where?" cried Mago, "Brother, I do not see what you intend to do. Rome has declared war and they will not be content to simply sit in Italy, waiting for us. We must get back to Carthage and prepare for the defense. Against her ancient walls the Roman legionaries will die in vain hope of victory!"

"No, Mago," grinned Hannibal. "We lost the first war by doing what the Romans expected. We met them in the middle and our forces crashed together. No, we must be smarter than them. We march north."

"To attack more cities? To extend the empire further? We are already at a stalemate in Iberia," Hasdrubal sounded incredulous. Again, Hannibal shook his head.

"My goal is victory at Rome, nothing less. We shall not win this war by attrition; our father lost his life doing that. We will invade Italy. And not just with foot soldiers. With cavalry, and archers, and elephants too!"

For a few moments, nothing could be heard but the snap of the flags in the wind and the rush of the waves on the shore.

"It's never been done!" whispered Hasdrubal, awe filling his voice.

"That's because the sons of Hamilcar Barca weren't there to do it!" Hannibal grasped his brothers by the shoulders. "Together, we shall bring Rome to its knees."

Thus began the long march. Elephants can cover ground as quickly as men can, and as they journeyed up through Iberia and into Gaul, the local tribes joined them. "Good!" smiled Hannibal, "For too long have your people suffered from Roman aggression. With our combined strength, nothing can stop us!"

But even Hasdrubal and Mago, who would have followed their brother into the gates of the Underworld itself, felt doubt settling on their hearts as the mighty Alps loomed before them, like a wall built not by giants but by the very gods themselves. "Do not despair!" shouted Hannibal as the snow whipped his face. "Wrap yourselves in cloaks and put blankets on the elephants. There are valleys and passes even in the Alps!"

In Rome, Fabius kept an eye on the south, watching for the tell-tale signs of an approaching army: dust from the thousands of feet and hooves, smoke from the burning of villages and towns. But day followed day, and he saw nothing. Scouts reported back; no sign of the Carthaginian fleet had been seen. And doubt came into Fabius' mind. "Was I wrong?" he wondered, "Must we reach out our fists and invade?" It was only then that a messenger came but from the north, not the south.

"A Carthaginian army has crossed the Alps!" he gasped, bent over double from running. "They have cavalry and elephants, and they have allied with the Gallic tribes!"

Fabius clutched at the chair in front of him, his eyes wide. "Inform the consul Sempronius Longus!" he barked, "He must bring his legions north at once!"

When Longus finally caught up with Hannibal's army, he was convinced that this brash but ingenious Carthaginian general had made a fatal error. Not only had Hannibal arrived in Italy as winter was closing in, but now, on the banks of the river Trebia, he had sent a large contingent of Numidan horsemen to harass the Roman army as it advanced. "See there?" he said, pointing across the wide valley. "The fool has over-committed his cavalry. They've crossed the river Trebia. Send a full attack!" With hoarse cries, the centurions urged their soldiers onward. Each man was armed with a helmet, breastplate, a thick, oval shield, a sword and a spear. They were supported by archers and javelin-throwers, and on their flanks stormed their cavalry, their bright helmets flashing in the sun. "Mars favors us!" intoned the consul proudly, urging his horse forward. "Bring me my shield, today, I shall wet my blade with the blood of Carthage!"

But across the river, Hannibal was watching the Romans advance. "That fool is responding just as I thought he would," he told Hasdrubal. "Take your cavalry to the outer wings and prepare to sweep around when I give the order." For Hannibal had arrayed his army in this way: in the center stood his Gallic allies, and outside of them stood his own spearmen, with archers behind them with taught bows. On the flanks stood the monstrous elephants, their tusks gleaming and their great ears flapping. The Numidian cavalry he had sent across the river had done its job of tempting the Romans to give chase and then cross the river.

Despite his life-long hatred for Rome, Hannibal had to admit that they had trained their soldiers well, for even as they struggled through the marsh on the banks of the Trebia, they held their line fairly well. "Let them come!" he ordered, and his grin broadened as the Romans, terrified by the hulking elephants on his flanks, funneled towards his center. "They hope to split our line and send us screaming into the woods," he muttered, "but soon they shall see."

The two armies crashed together, and Hannibal watched with detached, professional interest as the heavily armed legionaries of Rome tore through the Gallic tribesmen. "Have I over-estimated the Gauls or underestimated Rome?" he wondered, "It does not matter." Raising his hand, he signaled not to Hasdrubal, but to his other brother, Mago.

Mago, with a contingent of crack troops, had lain hidden on a small island in the middle of the river Trebia. Now, seeing Hannibal's sign, they rose up and sprinted across the ford, covering the space behind the Roman army in moments and falling on the legionaries like a pack of wolves. With deafening roars, the elephants charged, crushing men underfoot and rolling up the Roman battleline. Without space to move, the Romans could do nothing but flee or die.

Sempronius had not even had time to don his helmet. Turning his horse, he cried to his men to retreat as best they could, fleeing back across the Trebia, leaving thousands of their comrades lying dead. Looking over his shoulder, he saw a tall, dark man sitting on a black horse just behind the Carthaginians. Something about the man sent a cold chill down the consul's spine, "This nightmare is only just beginning."

CHAPTER 2: DEFEATS AND DELAYS

F ollowing the disastrous defeat at the river Trebia, Sempronius Longus, the consul, returned to Rome in utter disgrace. Luckily for him, his year as consul was soon over, two new magistrates, Gaius Flaminius and Spurius Carvilius, were elected. Not even Hannibal was daring enough to wage war during the frozen months, and thus both sides had time to rest, awaiting the warm spring mornings. Gaius, a hot-headed career-politician, was eager to drive the Carthaginians from the land. And so, as soon as the snow had melted, he raised a fresh army and set off to patrol the center of Italy. "The barbarians must be hungry after the long cold," he mused. "They will soon strike south to pillage what they can. And I shall be waiting for them."

Flaminius was half-right. Hannibal did lead his army south, but the Carthaginians did far more than steal food. They burnt whole villages, destroyed orchards, and sent thousands of Italians fleeing for their lives. But although the consul and his army chased Hannibal, they simply couldn't catch him. Enraged at the Carthaginian's cunning, Flaminius marched his men ever faster and finally closed in on the shores of a great lake: Trasimene. Hardly daring to believe it, Gaius would have sung for joy, but like a good Roman consul, he maintained a steady, poised manner. Hannibal's army had camped on the northern shore of Lake Trasimene, and Flaminius pitched his camp to the west of it. "The fool!" he snorted, "Can he not see that the hills curve around the lake to the east, penning him in? We march at dawn and shall fall upon them as they are dragging themselves from their beds."

Morning dawned, and Flaminius donned his best armor. "I shall lead the men into battle!" he called, and with a harsh screech of metal on metal, drew his sword. "Forth men, When I give the signal, charge them at the run and show them how real men fight!" It was, Gaius thought, the most glorious moment in his career: 25,000 men at his back, creeping along the shore of the lake in the grey, early morning light. Ahead, he could see the campfires burning low. "They don't even have sentries!" he hissed. Looking back, he saw the long line of men, like a great red and bronze snake along between the edge of the lake and the dark forest to their left. Rising to his full height he cried aloud. But his was not the only voice that sounded. From the trees, horns blew, and for a moment, Flaminius thought that the whole hillside was crashing down upon them. But it was not so. Thousands of Carthaginian and Gallic soldiers were charging down the slope. "Form ranks!" Gaius screamed, "Turn! Turn! From the trees!" But, out of the shadows, arrows came pouring down. One smote the consul in the chest, piercing his beautiful, shiny armor. Collapsing to his knees, the light dimming around him, Gaius could only watch as Hannibal's troops thundered into his own, driving them back into the freezing water of lake Trasimene. Then all went black.

There was total uproar in the Senate. Only a handful of Flaminius' legionaries had survived to limp back to Rome, bearing the dismal news. "We must raise a new army!" cried some of the senators.

"Flaminius must be avenged!" cried others.

"Fools!" boomed Fabius Maximus, and silence fell. Fabius glanced at the remaining consul, but Spurius looked pale and frightened, and just nodded meekly. "Fellow senators. Sempronius Longus lost 30,000 men to Hannibal. Flaminius lost a further 25,000 along with his own life. How many more good Romans must we send to this wolf?"

"What do you suggest," cried Minucius Rufus, an old rival of Fabius, "should we buy this barbarian off? Send him back with half the treasury and pray to the gods that he doesn't come again next year?"

Fabius ignored the interruption, and Rufus went red with anger.

"The Carthaginians are fighting in a way we have never seen before," continued Fabius. "Twice now they have lured us into a battle of their choosing, and twice they have crushed us. We must stop playing their game, or soon we shall have elephants in the forum, not in the Alps! I have a plan, my friends. It is not one many will like, but it is one I think will win."

Spurius the consul stepped forward. "I am still consul," he said, "but these are dark and desperate times. I call upon Fabius Maximus, twice a consul of Rome, to take up the dictatorship. He shall have all emergency powers to command for a six-month period. Let him drive this menace into the sea!"

"Aye!" cried the senators, raising their hands into the air.

And thus, Fabius Maximus was made dictator, and he immediately put his plan into action. He did not, however, sally forth as Longus or Flaminius had done. Sending out swift scouts and small, agile contingents, he harried Hannibal's army, but did not engage him directly in battle. Commanding such a large force, the son of Hamilcar had to raid and pillage, but so effective was Fabius' strategy, that he could not strike when and where he wished.

"This is not how Romans fight!" growled Minucius. "We strike hard and fast with the fist of our mighty legions. We don't prance about, avoiding the fight. Are you a coward, Fabius?"

But Fabius' reply was calm, "The Carthaginians have elephants and the best cavalry in the western world. This is a fact. We cannot face them in open battle. Hannibal has already proven this twice. I tell you, he is the greatest military mind Rome has yet faced. So instead, we shall wear him down. He is far from home, and our ships control the seas. Soon his men shall starve, his allies shall abandon him, and his army will collapse. That is how we shall win this war."

Months went by, and while Fabius' strategy kept Hannibal pinned to the highlands, still there was no sign of the Carthaginian army breaking apart. As the shock of the defeats at Trebia and Trasimene died down, the grumbling and the whispers grew once more. Spurius's year as consul came to an end, and the new consuls, Terentius Varro and Aemilius Paullus, had Maximus removed from the dictatorship. Fabius did not argue with them. "I serve Rome, not history," he said, "let those in later years say what they will. I know that I did what I thought was right."

Hannibal's men were starving. His allies, the Gauls, were grumbling, and even his brothers Hasdrubal and Mago were beginning to wonder how long they could maintain this campaign. But Hannibal was certain. "We shall strike south, away from Rome. The Romans are great fighters, but they have no patience. Their resolve will crumble, and they shall chase after us like the pack of wolves they are." Silently, Hannibal prayed that he was right. For all his outward confidence, the great general was shaken by the cold precision of the Roman dictator's strategy. "If I lose this campaign," he said to himself, "it will be because of Fabius' strategy."

On the eastern coast of Italy lay Cannae, a rich area of fine farms. Outside of Sicily, this was Rome's greatest source of grain. Filling their bags and their bellies, the Carthaginians raided, confident that they were far enough away from Rome to strike. What they did not realize was the true reason for the lack of the swift, harrying companies, which before had tormented them like flies around a bear. The answer came in the late morning: one of Hannibal's scouts tore along the track and into the camp. Hurling himself from the saddle, the man cried aloud to the general, "The Romans are coming!"

Hannibal smiled; Fabius' strategy was at an end. "How many?"

The scout gulped, his eyes wide, "Eight legions, and they have roused their Italian allies, who have sent a further 14,000 in horse- and foot-soldiers."

For the first time in his life, Hannibal Barca did not know what to say. The Romans had never committed more than four legions to the field throughout their entire history. This was the largest force they had ever assembled. And his men were tired. They had lost their last elephants during the winter. Maybe he had 50,000 men against the Romans' 85,000. It seemed hopeless. "I have never run from a fight," he said, raising his voice to address the assembled soldiers. "And nor have I lost one. Let us prepare for glory!"

The two consuls, Terentius Varro and Aemilius Paulus shared confident smiles as their huge ranks of soldiers marched forward. The Carthaginians had spread their infantry line in a shallow bowed shape, attempting to avoid being outflanked by the much larger Roman force. The cavalry from both sides dominated the wings, and as the two armies came together, the screams of horses could be heard even from this distance. "See," grinned Paulus, "Already our legionaries are pushing them back!"

But despite this promising start, things were going wrong on the wings. Hannibal's cavalry had already routed the Romans' allied horsemen and as the legionaries advanced, many tripped over the dead bodies that had fallen before them. The Carthaginians gave back further, forming an inverted crescent, like a terrible moon filled with swords and spears and shields. Crushed together, the soldiers of Rome found their lines breaking, and their enemies scythed through the gaps. Varro and Paulus could only watch with horror as their huge army collapsed upon itself, the Carthaginian cavalry sweeping around to hem them in. Drawing his sword Paulus cried aloud and charged. It was the last brave thing he ever did.

By the end of the day, perhaps 50,000 legionaries lay on the dusty ground. Varro had escaped with few more than 4,000 men – just half a legion. The rest had fled or been captured. "Truly," said Varro as he scrambled northwards, "this is Rome's darkest day."

CHAPTER 3: THE LONG STALEMATE

Few had thought that Rome could suffer a greater defeat than the battle of Lake Trasimene, but Hannibal had proved them wrong at Cannae. With another consul and at least 50,000 Roman legionaries dead, there seemed to be no stopping the Carthaginians. Winter brought fresh snow and biting wind, and Hannibal wintered in the south of Italy. His men, though cold, were in high spirits. "There are no more armies left to fight!" they cried joyfully. "Italy is as good as ours."

In Hannibal's tent, however, an argument raged over what to do next.

"Why have we not already marched on Rome?" cried Hasdrubal, one of Hannibal's brothers. "Their legions have been destroyed or scattered to the winds, their leaders have been slain, their morale has been crushed. This is the time to complete our victory!"

But Hannibal, strangely, shook his head, "Our supply lines are still weak, brother. We must build alliances. I foresee a future when Italy sits in the arms of our empire, but we cannot win this war with blood alone."

Shocking the rest of the commanders, Hasdrubal's eyes blazed, "You know how to win a battle, brother, but you have no clue how to use a victory!"

Meanwhile in Rome, the mood in the Senate was sober and angry. The surviving consul, Varro, was in total disgrace, and did not say a word throughout the proceedings. Many senators were shouting, but few were agreeing. At last, Fabius Maximus made his voice heard once more.

"My fellow senators, I am not one to gloat, but did I not tell you it was foolish to meet this man in open battle? But do not forget that we are Romans, children of Romulus, the very son of Mars, god of war. We shall not go quietly into this African night! Raise up more armies. Take any man of fighting age, no matter if he is a criminal or a slave. Give him a sword and a shield."

"And do what?" cried his opponents.

"Invade," the voice of a tall, young man in military uniform broke through the raucous voices of the proud senators. He was Publius Cornelius Scipio, one of the few survivors of Cannae. He was young, a junior senator and officer in Varro's army, but he stood tall and strong before the older men.

"We have forces in the other provinces," he said, gesturing north and west. "In Gaul and Iberia. Let us put them to use. Fabius speaks wisely, we must raise whatever forces we can here in Italy, but now is the time to take the fight to Carthage. Hannibal is far from home, and our navy still controls the seas. We must divide his forces and his support. This is a war that will consume the Mediterranean. Some of you will say this is too risky. But I say to you: Fortune favors the brave."

Thus it was, with grudging support, that Scipio began his campaign. Fabius raised what forces he could in Italy and continued his war of attrition in Italy. Meanwhile, Publius went to Iberia, collecting troops from the garrisons along the way, as well as from allied city-states. Young though he was, he showed incredible military skill, marching deep into Carthaginian territory. Raging at the return of the Fabian strategy and the second danger to his supply lines, Hannibal sent his own brothers, Hasdrubal and Mago, back to Iberia to counter Scipio.

And so began the long stalemate. Hannibal had managed to bring many Italian cities over to his side, and with their help, he captured several more, but wherever he and his army weren't, Fabius swooped in and retook what he had taken. Refusing to give battle, Fabius infuriated his Carthaginian foe. But neither side could gain the upper hand. Meanwhile, Hasdrubal, Mago and Scipio fought a bloody war in Iberia. For years the conflict dragged on, with Hasdrubal himself falling in battle against Scipio's Iberian allies. The death of his brother brought about a terrible, reckless change in Mago Barca. Calling for reinforcements from Africa, Mago actively sought out Scipio. "This war has gone on long enough," the youngest son of Hamilcar seethed.

It was at Ilipa in southern Iberia that Hamilcar caught up with Scipio's legions. Thanks to the timely arrival of more troops from Africa, Mago's forces outnumbered the Romans considerably. As with Hannibal's army back in Italy, Mago knew that his cavalry was superior to those Scipio had on the field. "And I have war elephants!" he smiled, "No Roman army has survived against them. It is time to turn the tables on this Roman upstart! Tomorrow will be the day when the name of Mago rises to rival that of Hannibal!"

But the next day brought unwelcome surprises to the Carthaginians. As the sun broke over the hills to the east, light cavalry and javelin-throwers fell upon Mago's camp, killing several and waking the army with their noise. Mago, enraged, ordered his men to arm themselves even before they had had time to eat. "This Roman is trying to do something clever!" he told them, pacing up and down in excitement. "But he shall fail. I know the Roman battle order. They shall advance on us with their strongest troops in the center and their allies on the wings. In so doing, they will attempt to break our line apart."

Therefore, Mago drew up his own line to mirror the Romans', with his cavalry on the wings and his war elephants out in front.

But Scipio did not advance. Instead, he sent his cavalry and light skirmishers forward and harried the Carthaginian troops. Ever impatient, Mago ordered his elephants to charge. "Send them screaming back to Italy!" he cried.

Across the plain, Scipio smiled, for his enemy was acting just as he had planned. "Spears!" he shouted, "Strike the great brutes before they reach our lines!" With astonishing speed and skill, the Roman cavalry fell upon the elephants, stabbing and cutting at their thick, grey skin. With deafening roars, the monsters lashed out with trunk and tusk, but they could not keep pace with the swift hooves of the horses. As the sandy soil turned red with their blood, the elephants, maddened with pain and rage, turned and ran back into their own army's line. With sickening crunches, the beasts tore gaps into the Carthaginians' own line, killing dozens as they rampaged away from the swords and spears of the cavalry.

"Forward, Romans!" called Publius, "Forth to victory!"

Mago was yelling, trying to bring his troops back into line when the Roman legions struck. But, to Mago's horror, he saw that Scipio's infantry was not laid out as he had expected. The heavily armed legionnaires were arrayed on the flanks, with the Iberian allies holding the middle ground. "Kill them!" he cried, "kill them all!" But it was too late. Already, Scipio's troops were rolling up with Carthaginian line, pushing them back in on themselves, just as Hannibal's troops had routed the Romans at Cannae.

Back in Italy, Hannibal received the news of his brother's defeat with grim weariness. He had lost one of his eyes to a terrible infection some years back, but his remaining eye still blazed with the same fire.

"Where did they find this Scipio?" he growled, screwing the letter up and hurling it in the fire.

CHAPTER 4: ZAMA & THE FALL OF HANNIBAL

In an instant, the tide of the second great war between Carthage and Rome had turned. Mago Barca had lost a great army at Ilipa in Iberia, and now the legions of Rome had one name on their lips: Publius Cornelius Scipio. With the brother of Hannibal defeated, the war in Iberia was swiftly brought to a close, chasing the Carthaginians out of the peninsula. With such a triumph behind him, Publius turned his eyes on an even greater prize: Carthage itself. But he was not a consul. He had been awarded proconsular power and rank by the Senate in order to command the campaign in Iberia, but with that victory won, he now had to return to Rome.

Striding into the high-ceilinged Senate hall, Scipio could not help but grin sheepishly as all the senators applauded him. He could well remember how many of them had whispered behind their hands when he had left for Iberia. No-one whispered now, all shouted his praise. Raising his hand for silence, he addressed the assembled senators.

"The war in Iberia is won, but still Hannibal darkens the land. Despite our best efforts, our finest soldiers, and the leadership of

Fabius Maximus," here he bowed to the elder statesman and general, who had guided the Senate through this war with his wise strategy, "we are no closer to ridding ourselves of this menace, this nightmare. He has taken cities throughout the south of Italy, he has allies across the land, but still he has not attacked Rome. Why is a mystery, but from this silence comes wisdom: We must invade Carthage, for that alone will draw Hannibal away from Italy. Thus far he has proved invincible on Italian soil, perhaps the same will be true for Romans on Carthaginian soil!"

The invasion of Africa had not been attempted since the first war with Carthage. And while Rome's navy was now the undisputed master of the seas, it was still a bold and dangerous venture. Within days of arriving on the shores of Africa, Scipio learned that Hannibal too had arrived. "How does he know every move we make?" the imperator whispered, feeling doubt for the first time. "We must find a battlefield of our choosing, not his."

And find it, they did; at Zama. Perhaps twenty miles inland, it is a barren plain of rocks and sand. The legionaries did not like it at all, but Scipio saw there the canvas on which he would paint his greatest victory. "Listen here, my brothers of the sword!" he proclaimed, "Though we are on alien soil, the day shall be ours!" And then he explained his plan.

The day was dry and breezy, and on the wind the trumpeting calls of war elephants could be heard. Scipio's legionaries stood in their carefully arranged formation, shields overlapped, their spears at the ready. Through the haze of warm air, they saw the army of Carthage approaching. As ever, Hannibal had arrayed his war elephants before his infantry, with the cavalry on the wings. Scipio had taken up position in the front rank, and confident as he was in his plan, even he felt the blood leave his cheeks as those huge grey beasts came ever closer. Looking to his left and right, he called down the line, "Remember, hold the line until my signal!"

An African war elephant is a terrible sight to behold. Standing twice as tall again as the tallest man, their gleaming white tusks can kill a man with a single thrust, and they can simply crush a shield. But Scipio had a plan. As the elephants' riders goaded them forward, the beasts roared and trumpeted, but the legionaries stood firm. With meters to go, Scipio cried "Now!" And the front ranks of the Roman battle line split, allowing the elephants to run straight through. Behind them, in the classic Roman layout of serried ranks, Scipio had arranged his men in columns, down which the elephants thundered. Hundreds of spears were jabbed into their thick hides. Arrows were loosed, javelins were hurled. Within moments, nearly every elephant Hannibal had was either dead or fleeing back the way they had come. "Forth, cavalry!" Shouted Scipio, signaling to his horsemen. With a tumult of hooves, the Roman cavalry charged, shepherding the remaining elephants directly into the path of the Carthaginian cavalry.

"Legions of Rome, reform!" ordered Scipio, and with a great tramping of feet, the infantry reformed their battleline. "Advance!"

Hannibal may have lost his elephants and his cavalry was beset, but he still out-numbered the Romans. With a grim expression, he dismounted and took up his place in the infantry line. "For Carthage!"

The battle lasted all day. Those who survived said it was like the stories of Homer but told anew and fresh. Both sides fought with fire and fury, and the day would not have gone Scipio's way had his cavalry not been victorious on the wings and swooped around behind the Carthaginians. But Rome finally took the day. Hannibal escaped alive, but his myth was dead. Unlike his rival, Scipio did not hesitate to press his advantage and marched on Carthage. There, he negotiated their surrender, but he was gracious in victory. The terms were not terrible, and the Carthaginian Adirim bowed to his wishes. And thus the second war between Carthage and Rome came to an end.

It so happened that, perhaps six years later, Scipio returned to Carthage, but not with an army. Relations between the two powers had cooled, and while they would never be friends, there was a sense of respect felt by both sides. Leaving the hall of the Adirim, he heard someone calling his name. Turning, he saw a tall man with grey in his beard and only one eye. A chill hand rested on his heart. "Hannibal Barca?" he asked, wishing he had brought a weapon with him, but the old general smiled. "Indeed. And I hear, now, that they call you Scipio Africanus?"

Scipio blushed slightly, "It wasn't my idea."

"Come, let us have a drink – the day is too hot."

One drink became several, and the evening closed in as the two former enemies discussed the finer points of leadership and tactics. "Who, then," asked Scipio, "in your mind was the greatest general?" He expected Hannibal to name himself but was surprised at the answer.

"Alexander the Great of Macedon, of course," came the swift reply. "He conquered half the known world. I think we are both glad that he never decided to go west instead of east, or we would all be speaking Greek!"

"Fine," conceded Scipio, "I agree with you. But who then is the second greatest?"

Again, without hesitation, Hannibal replied, "Pyrrhus of Epirus. He was more daring even than Alexander, and a general must be brave."

Scipio laughed, "And I suppose you would put yourself as the third greatest, then?"

Hannibal smiled, his lone eye glinting. "Of course, who else? I alone, other than Hercules, son of Zeus, have led an army across the mighty Alps. I brought"

"Well," Scipio sipped his drink, "I did defeat you. If I hadn't where would you rank yourself?"

Hannibal smiled more broadly. "In that case, I would be considered greater even than Alexander!"

Scipio blinked and sat there stunned as the full weight of the compliment Hannibal had paid him rolled over him.

"You know," he said, finally finding his voice, "I may be called Africanus, but now the people of Rome cry 'Hannibal is at the gates!' whenever something truly terrible happens. You have changed us forever: no enemy of Rome ever tormented us for so long. You were our greatest nightmare."

The old Carthaginian sighed, "And yet, I fear I must always live my life looking over my shoulder. I was the enemy of Rome, and there is no worse foe than the one you have defeated. Your people have no patience, and I don't think your city will sleep soundly until this old man has gone to his grave."

Rising to his feet, he offered Scipio his hand. The two men embraced and went their separate ways, for their war was now over.

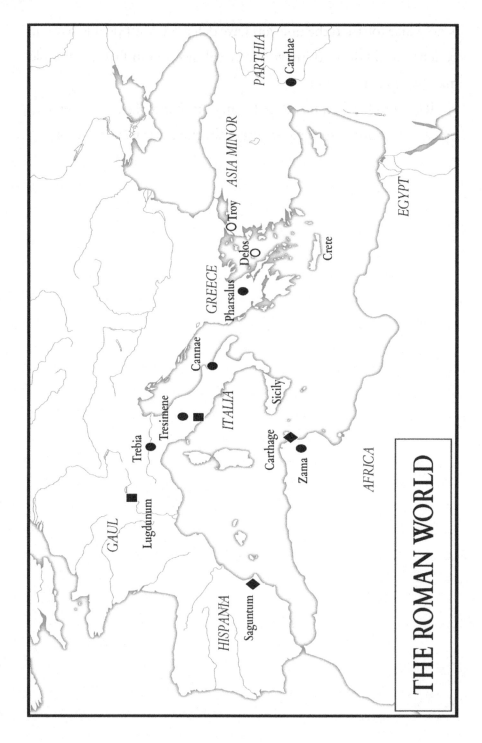

THE ROMAN WORLD

Part IV

Julius Caesar

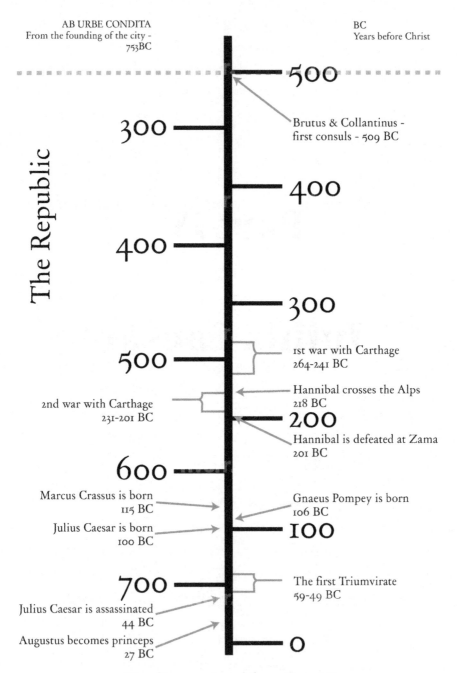

AB URBE CONDITA
From the founding of the city -
753BC

BC
Years before Christ

The Republic

500

300

Brutus & Collantinus -
first consuls - 509 BC

400

400

300

500

1st war with Carthage
264-241 BC

2nd war with Carthage
231-201 BC

Hannibal crosses the Alps
218 BC

200

Hannibal is defeated at Zama
201 BC

600

Marcus Crassus is born
115 BC

Gnaeus Pompey is born
106 BC

Julius Caesar is born
100 BC

100

700

The first Triumvirate
59-49 BC

Julius Caesar is assassinated
44 BC

Augustus becomes princeps
27 BC

0

Timeline continued from Page 57.

CHAPTER I: THE TRIUMVIRATE

It was the 694th year since the founding of Rome, for so the people of that city reckoned their calendar. In that time the small village founded by Romulus on the Palatine had grown into a mighty city. That city had fielded great legions of disciplined soldiers that were now feared across the known world. It had thrust out its arms and conquered the whole of Italy and even beyond. Now the Republic, as the Romans called themselves, governed provinces in Iberia, southern Gaul, Greece, and even had footholds along the coast of North Africa. Rome's success was due not only to its legions but to great individuals, particularly its cunning and clever generals. Without the likes of Scipio Africanus, Rome would never have defeated Hannibal of Carthage. Now, in early January, three of its greatest military leaders were meeting in one house just north of the Palatine hill in Rome.

The owner of the house, Gaius Julius Caesar, was the youngest, with a slim, hard face and piercing blue eyes. He had welcomed his older ally, Marcus Licinius Crassus, with a cup of wine and a winning smile. "Marcus! It has been too long!" The older statesman accepted the cup gladly and lounged by the fire with a sigh. "It's cold out, Gaius. Why you felt it necessary to meet tonight of all nights...?" his voice trailed off as he heard the front door open and close once more.

Caesar smiled and bowed, "All shall become clear once I have welcomed my second guest." Within moments, he had returned, and Crassus nearly dropped his wine cup as he leaped to his feet, surprise and rage twisting his lined features. The third man was Gnaeus Pompey, Crassus' lifelong political enemy. Neither agreed on when their rivalry had begun, but both argued that it was the other's fault. Even when they had served together as the two consuls, the joint heads of the Roman Republic, they had spent as much time bickering as they had governing.

"What is he doing here?" cried Crassus and Pompey in unison. "I'm not staying if he is!"

Julius laughed, "That may be the first time you have agreed on something. But neither of you is going anywhere until you've heard me out."

To Crassus' great surprise, Pompey relented and reclined on a couch opposite him. Caesar took up the third couch between the two of them. Julius took a deep sip of wine, a deep breath and then began. "Gnaeus, there are those in Rome who call you 'the Great', like the Macedonian Alexander, because of your astounding career. I would number myself among those people." Then he turned to Crassus, "Marcus, you are the richest man in Rome, some say, and your voice reverberates through the hallowed hall of the Senate. People listen when you speak."

The cup of wine shattered as Caesar slammed his fist down on the table, his eyes on fire, "But all three of us have been thwarted by lesser men! Gnaeus, you want to reward our brave legionaries with pensions when they retire, a noble cause. Marcus, how long have we talked about reducing the debts of the farmers across Italy without whom we would all starve? You have both been consuls," he paused for a moment, eying with some jealousy the purple edging on his guests' togas, symbols of their previous honor, "and without us three, the Republic would be far smaller and much less safe than it is now. Who drove the pirates from the Mediterranean?" he pointed at Pompey, "Who crushed the slave revolt of Spartacus?" he gestured to Crassus. "Who doubled our great Republic's holdings in Iberia?" he jabbed himself in the chest. Gnaeus and Marcus glanced at each other, then back to Gaius. Pompey ventured a word as Caesar breathed slowly, regaining his composure.

"That's politics, Gaius, that's life. We can't have everything we want."

Caesar shook his head, "That's where you are wrong. If we combine our resources, our connections, our popularity, no-one could stand against us. If we stop fighting amongst ourselves, we could change Rome for the better, for who better than us to guide our glorious Republic?"

For the first time that any of them could remember, small smiles bloomed slowly across the faces of both Pompey and Crassus. Looking at each other once more, Pompey remarked, "If he can make us agree, there's no stopping him!"

Marcus laughed, "Except us. That's the beauty and balance of this: With an alliance of two, conflict will always emerge. But with a trio it is different: One will always be outvoted, or there will be total agreement! But let us keep this triumvirate secret as best we can."

"Agreed," chorused Gnaeus and Gaius.

And thus it was that these three men, who had so often been at loggerheads, finally forged an alliance of shadows. With the support of his new allies, Caesar was elected as one of the next year's two consuls. With their ally in such a powerful position, able to decide what should be debated in the Senate and to choose what laws should be put to the vote, Crassus and Pompey both succeeded where they had so long failed. Pompey's veterans were awarded pensions, the first time any soldiers had been awarded money after retirement. And thanks to Crassus, the farmers of Italy no longer had to fear the debt-collectors, for their repayable loans were now cut in half. These measures made all three men very popular, and together they rode the waves of public admiration. They did not always agree, but as Marcus had so wisely noted: two always allied themselves, and so the third had to go along with their plan. Their disagreements were always in private, for they never met openly, lest their rivals realize what they were doing. Thus, if Pompey did not like the idea, Caesar and Crassus overrode him, and if Gaius could not persuade his two elder partners, they overrode him. It was as perfect an arrangement as could be imagined, for them at least.

On one point there was total unity amongst the triumvirate: As Caesar's yearlong consulship came to a close, he wanted to return to the campaign. And if Gaius was to gain glory and riches by conquering new lands, so too should Marcus and Gnaeus. Thus, it was agreed that Caesar would take his legions and strike north into Gaul, and Pompey would expand the Republic's provinces in North Africa, joining their lands in Egypt and Carthage with the lands by the Pillars of Hercules. Crassus, meanwhile, would march east and take on the Parthian Empire, which was beginning to raid their provinces once more. "For five years, we shall go our separate ways," declared Gaius during their last meeting before the three were due to depart on the campaign. "And when we return, Rome shall be brighter and richer and greater than when we left it. May Mars, god of war and victory in battle, watch over us all."

A year had passed since the triumvirate had left Rome and Pompey, though he loved being on campaign, was not happy. His disquiet came not from the irritations of handling troops on the march – he had been doing that for most of his life – nor from the terrible heat of the African sun. No, he had received a letter from an old ally of his, Marcus Cicero, which worried him greatly.

"My dear Pompey,

I am full of admiration when I hear of your exploits on our southern borders. Alas, however, I am one of the few who knows of them. For Caesar's supporters make sure that the people of Rome hear only about his victories against the Gallic barbarians. Those of us who champion your cause do our best, but I fear that we are being outflanked. Certainly, Caesar has conquered many lands and has sent much gold back to Rome already, so that games in the arena are held at his expense. The poor people love free entertainment, and so the name of Gaius Julius Caesar is on many lips. If there is anything you can do to rival this man's popularity, I beseech you to do so, for otherwise you will return to Rome and no-one will remember your name, despite your glory and many years of service.

Faithfully,

Marcus."

Pompey crumpled the letter from his old friend and tossed it angrily into the fire. "Cicero is many things," Gnaeus said to himself. "A lawyer, a politician, a philosopher, and a coward, at least in battle.

But he is not a fool, indeed he is the wisest man I know. If he says there is a problem, then I had best listen to him."

What he should do, Pompey wasn't certain, but the next day, another letter arrived, not from Rome, but from Carrhae on the border with the Parthian Empire. This letter, though he didn't realize it, would alter the course of history. "What does Crassus have to report?" wondered Pompey, unrolling the thick parchment. But his old rival had nothing to report. Indeed, Marcus Licinius Crassus, so his primary tribune wrote with a quavering hand, would never put pen to parchment again. The man who had once been called the richest in Rome, who had fought many wars and won many victories, was dead, killed in battle.

This letter was not crumpled up or tossed into the fire. It fell from Pompey's hand as he held his shaking palms to his eyes, the enormity of this news crashing down upon him in waves. Crassus was gone, which meant the Eastern frontier was no longer safe. But at that moment, such worries meant little to Pompey. "Caesar will know of this soon," he muttered, "and when he does he shall return to Rome, not in mourning but in triumph! The triumvirate has ended, and it is Caesar versus Pompey now. I must convince the Senate that Gaius is a threat to the Republic, for otherwise he shall do the same to me!"

The letter containing the news of Crassus' death crunched underfoot as Pompey sprinted from his tent, shouting at his tribunes to have the legions break camp. "We return to Italy! Rome is in danger, even if it doesn't know it yet!"

Chapter 2: The Die is Cast

Gaius Julius Caesar, commander of the legions of Gaul, former consul of Rome, and one of the two remaining triumvirs, looked out over his winter camp at Lugdunum. Ordered rows of tents spread out for nearly a mile, for he had called together half his forces: The Seventh and Eighth Legions, two of his most experienced, were present, as were the Thirteenth and the Sixth. Four others he had sent under the command of a favorite former tribune, Marcus Antonius, further north. The remaining three were garrisoned throughout Gaul, for he could not risk his newly conquered provinces rebelling while he was away.

"News from Rome, Imperator!" called Decimus Brutus, another of Gaius' tribunes, marching smartly up to where the commander sat. Presenting Caesar with the still-sealed letter, Brutus stepped back and stood by the tent-flap, awaiting any further orders. Gaius half-smiled as he broke the wax seal and studied the contents. As he read, the smile faded, and a frown furrowed his brow. "Unexpected news, sir?" Brutus asked, watching Caesar's expression intently.

"Bad news, but not unexpected," the Imperator replied. "The Senate has declared my command at an end. They are summoning me back to face trial for treason. Many of the most senior senators have spoken out against me: Cicero, no surprises there, and Cato, Bibulus," he ticked the names off on his fingers, "and your brother: Marcus." Decimus gasped and took a step back before remembering his place and snapping to attention again. "Do we have a problem, Decimus?" Caesar's tone was light, but his eyes were hard. "Marcus is the head of your family, where he leads, you should follow. Speak your mind without fear, tribune."

Brutus paused for a long moment, "Imperator, I swore an oath to serve the Republic, not my brother. I won't be the only man here with brothers or cousins or friends standing against you, but you are my Imperator. The Senate is full of old men who know nothing of the frontier, nothing of the challenges we face. If it were not for your leadership, Gauls would be crawling over the Alps and plundering the green fields of Italy. I stand with you until the end."

Caesar smiled as he stood to face the young man. "Well spoken, Decimus. But what of Pompey? My informant tells me that if I refuse the summons, he will lead the Senate's army and bring me back to Rome. Surely he knows the challenges we face? He was carving out new frontiers before you were even born."

Decimus frowned, as though he suspected a trap, "My brother said that Pompey always wanted more recognition, more praise. Our families are both old and respected, but it was never enough for Pompey. That's why, even when his hair turned grey, he still wanted to lead armies. That's all this is for him: more glory. You want to make Rome greater than ever before. That's the difference between you and him, Imperator."

Caesar laughed. "I should have you write my speeches for me, Decimus! Cicero would take notes from you. But don't fetch your ink pot just yet. Tomorrow, I will lead the Thirteenth Legion south. You will command the remaining legions and follow in two days. Follow the coast south to Rome. I shall meet you there."

He turned away, leaving Decimus gaping. After a moment, the young tribune found his voice. "But where are you going, Imperator? What are you going to do?"

Gaius sighed as he tapped the rolled letter on the desk in front of him. "I'm going to cast the die, Decimus. I'm going to war."

When Marcus Tullius Cicero entered the Senate on that cold winter's day, there was a sense of foreboding the like of which he had rarely felt before. A tribune, his cloak and greaves splattered with mud from hard riding, stood to one side, his face grim and set. The two newly elected consuls, Gaius Claudius Marcellus and Lucius Cornelius Lentulus, stood and silence fell. "Senators," the voice of Marcellus rang clear in the high-ceilinged hall, "there is grave news from the north." He gestured to the military officer, "Our scouts report that Caesar has led a legion across the river Rubicon– the ancient boundary between Italy and Gaul. This violates the sacred truce of Italy: no army may be present here save at the Senate's direct invitation!"

A great hubbub of angry muttering arose, and at that moment, Cicero knew his time had come. Rising to his feet, he caught Marcellus' eye, and the consul bowed his head slightly.

"Friends!" called Cicero, raising his hand before him, "Our Republic is threatened. Not since the dark days of Hannibal the Carthaginian have we sensed such a specter of doom at our doorstep. Like that barbarian foe, Caesar has marched over the Alps, desecrating the land of Italy with his selfish invasion. Who shall take up arms against such a man, such a demon? We have legions loyal to the people of Rome. They must be marshaled. I do not ask for this honor, to defend the fatherland. Rather I ask that we entrust this duty to one far greater than I, than any of us here: Gnaeus Pompey. Caesar has conquered the scattered tribes of Gaul, but will he stand a chance against the legions of Rome, under our greatest general? What say you? Will Pompey lead our legions to victory?"

"Aye!" The thunder of the senator's voices was followed by their applause.

Gnaeus Pompey smiled and nodded his thanks to the great orator. Rising to his feet, his own hand in the air, he addressed his fellow senators, "Friends, I thank you. We Romans are accustomed to war, but it is a terrible thing to raise a sword against a fellow Roman. Let us never forget that it is Caesar who has pushed us to this moment. He has cast the die, but he shall find that the game has turned against him! I depart tomorrow, for battle, for victory, for the Republic!"

Months later, however, Pompey was far less confident. With astonishing speed that left him and the Senate's army standing, Caesar had zig-zagged across Italy, capturing Sicily, Rome's main supplier of grain, and gathering support and swelling his ranks with those who preferred him to Pompey. Gnaeus, knowing that a hungry army was doomed, had abandoned Rome, and taken his troops across the sea to Greece. A cat-and-mouse game ensued, with neither side wanting to commit to a full battle. But at Pharsalus on the banks of the Enipeus River, the armies of Caesar and Pompey finally faced each other across an open plain.

"Imperator!" Decimus Brutus marched into his general's tent and saluted. This time, Caesar was not alone, the commanders of his other legions, Marcus Antonius, Domitius Calvinus, and Cornelius Sulla were also present.

"Report." commanded Caesar, settling down in his chair with an expectant air.

Brutus laid a sketched map out on the desk. "Our scouts report that Pompey has pitched camp on the foothills of Mount Dogantzis and arrayed his army before it." He pointed to two points on the map. Gaius glanced down at it and then back up to his tribune.

"Is that all? How many times must I tell you, Decimus: In war details matter. How many? Where are they situated?"

Decimus swallowed, and then continued in clear, concise terms. "The Cicilian and Iberian Legions are formed up on the right flank, closest to the river. The center is made up of the three Syrian Legions, and the First and Third Legions make up the left of his infantry line. Approximately 38,000 troops. Perhaps 6,000 cavalry are stationed on his left wing, nearest to the open plain, and his Auxiliary archers and slingers are placed behind them."

Marcus Antonius whistled softly, his eyebrows disappearing into his long fringe.

"Imperator," Calvinus paused and then continued, "is it wise to offer battle here? We have more legions, but all of them are understrength, and our cavalry number at most 1,000 ready to fight. We should attempt to draw them into a chase and catch them on the march."

Sulla nodded, "Pompey has chosen this place for a reason. We should not give him the satisfaction."

All waited for Caesar to speak. To their astonishment, he was smiling.

"You all forget three things: First, our legions might be understrength, but they are the best in the world. These men have fought with me for nearly a decade. They are undefeated. Secondly, Pompey has to fight, or the Senate will take his command away from him. They have forced his hand, not ours. Thirdly, I know Pompey. I know how he thinks." And with a light in his eyes, he explained his battle plan. "Now go, sharpen your blades and order your legions!"

Confident of victory, Pompey waited for his rival to make the first move. With the river protecting his left flank, Caesar advanced, some of his best legions in the middle, with his small contingent of cavalry facing Pompey's superior force. The sun beat down and the men sweated in their armor. Their shields were heavy and the air was dry. But Gaius' legions did not waver as they approached; their shields overlapped like a solid wall. They had done this thousands of times before. At the last moment, the centurions barked their orders, and the front rank hurled their spears at Pompey's men, decimating the shield wall. With glitter-like stars in the sky, the legionaries of Caesar drew their short, stabbing swords and advanced, crashing into the Senate troops like thunderbolts.

Watching from behind, Gnaeus smiled. This had been his plan all along. Nodding to his cavalry commander, Labienus, he released the charge. 6,000 horsemen accelerated to a gallop, careering towards his rival's tiny band of riders. But at the last moment, Caesar's cavalry spurred aside, revealing what lay in wait: Veteran soldiers, each carrying a long spear. With hideous shrieks, the horses fell upon the long blades, twisting and flailing, their riders thrown, and the rest of the force driven mad with pain and fear. Then, Gaius' own cavalry struck, splintering the Senate's horsemen and sending them galloping from the battlefield.

Meanwhile, Pompey's less-experienced troops were cracking under the weight of Caesar's battle-hardened legionaries. With a stony precision, they stabbed and advanced, stabbed and advanced, and Pompey could do nothing but watch in horror as his army collapsed. Staring out over the heads of the battling soldiers, he saw Caesar himself, resplendent in his bright red cloak. Torn between rage and fear, Gnaeus turned to see the senators who had accompanied him to watch the victory were now mounting their own horses and fleeing. "Enough!" he cried, gesturing to his commanders. "Let no more Roman blood be spilled! The day is Caesar's!"

CHAPTER 3. THE IDES OF MARCH

Rome had seen many triumphs in its 700 hundred years, but few compared to the day when Gaius Julius Caesar returned following his defeat of the Senate. Those senators who had actively opposed him stood silent and fearful. Meanwhile those who had supported him rubbed their hands with glee, wondering what brutal or degrading punishments Caesar had in mind for his defeated enemies. Following his defeat at Pharsalus, Pompey had fled to Egypt, where he had been mysteriously murdered. With their champion gone, the Pompeian faction was divided and desperate.

With shining armor and a blood-red cloak, Gaius strode into the Senate, ostentatiously removing his sword before entering. The laurel crown of victory adorned his forehead, his smile was broad, but his eyes were watchful. No-one spoke as he stood in the middle of the room and gestured for all to sit.

"When a triumphant general returns to Rome," his voice rang through the dusty silence, "a slave stands behind him on his chariot, whispering to him, 'Remember, you are mortal.' I am no god; I am just a man. A man who has served Rome, its Senate, and its people his whole life." He stared around the room, making eye contact with many of the senior senators: Cicero, Cato, Marcus Brutus, Cassius Longinus, along with many others. "And so I shall continue to do so. There are some of you who fear my retribution. I say here today that you need have no such fear. Enough good Roman blood has already been spilled. I have fought enough wars for a lifetime, and I have no desire to harm or punish any of you.

"That said, I am no longer consul, and I do not wish to upset the orderly running of government by calling for a new election now. So I humbly," his smile broadened, "request that this sage body consider what is best for Rome, and give me emergency powers to restore the Republic to what it once was. The provinces I conquered in Gaul need further pacification and organization; the legions whose numbers have been sadly diminished must be brought back to full strength; the disquiet throughout our lands must be soothed by clarity and cohesion from us," he gestured to his fellow senators, "the wisest and best men in the whole Republic. Let us work together to keep this shining light of civilization burning brighter and brighter for all time!"

For a while, the fears the senators had held were hushed. Caesar had disappointed many of his followers, Marcus Antonius in particular, by not exacting revenge on those who had opposed him, but in doing so he had calmed the passions of the political elite. They had elected him to the dictatorship, a short-term office that gave him unlimited power to govern Rome. This he did, but mostly in consultation with the Senate. As the year drew to a close however, Caesar declared that there was still much work to be done. So popular was he with the people and so powerful was the faction of senators he controlled, that the vote to extend his dictatorship for another year was successful. The likes of Cato and Cicero began to mutter darkly once more.

Another year went by, and still Caesar did not give up his power. "The Gauls are proving more troublesome than I had hoped, and there are still threats to the east!" he told the senators. Dark looks were exchanged. Even Decimus Brutus, who had served Caesar for so long, started to have misgivings. Turning to his brother Marcus, he whispered, "He's still acting like he's a general on campaign: He gives orders and expects total obedience. That's fine when you're on the frontier, but this is Rome!"

Marcus nodded slowly, "Now you begin to see what we saw years ago, Decimus. But hush, lest Caesar's cronies hear us."

But as Caesar's rule kept getting extended, the mood in the Senate darkened still further. In the fifth year of his dictatorship, a motion was passed to give him power *in perpetuo*, for life. The evening after the vote, Marcus Brutus, his brother-in-law Cassius Longinus, and many other senators met in Brutus' house. Their faces were grim, their eyes downcast.

Marcus stepped forward, "My fellow senators, this is a dark day. What we have long feared has come to pass: Rome is now ruled by a king." A frisson went round the room. Brutus raised his chin. "It is strange that I stand here today. Five centuries ago, my forefather, Lucius Junius Brutus, was in a similar position and he did not hesitate. He did as all good Romans do and took action. Recognizing that Tarquin the Proud was destroying our great city, he cast him out. But what is not public knowledge is a tale that has been passed down in our family since that day: Two of Lucius' own sons plotted to restore Tarquin, and my ancestor had both of them executed! To my family, there is no higher purpose than the service of Rome. My sons are still young, but I will not have them live another year under the rule of this tyrant. My friends, Caesar must die!"

The day dawned bright and fine. Gaius Caesar called for the slaves to bring him a clean toga, and he smiled as he watched his adopted son, Octavian, lounging with a long scroll. "Is that my Gallic War commentary?" he asked, glancing at the title. "I thought you hated the idea of military service?"

Octavian looked up at his adopted father, "I'm eleven, what do I know? Besides, I can't avoid the army if I want to succeed in the Senate!"

Gaius ruffled the boy's hair. "Smart lad. I expect you to have read all seven books by the time I return."

"You're going on campaign again?"

Gaius nodded, "But first I must go the Senate. There are instructions I must give them before I leave."

"No!" A cry erupted behind him, and he turned to see his wife, Calpurnia, clasping her hands over her mouth.

"What is it, dearest?" Caesar asked, rushing to her.

"Please, don't go today," she begged, "I had a dream where I..." she choked back tears, "I saw your body, there was blood everywhere. Please, not today."

Gaius gave her a hug and smiled, "Don't worry – no-one would dare harm me! Besides, it is a holy day: the Ides of March, remember? I won't be long."

"Where is the Senate meeting today?" asked Octavian brightly. "Have the repairs to the senate-house finished yet?"

Caesar shook his head, a sudden thoughtful look on his face. "No, today we meet at the Curia of Pompey," he sighed sadly, reminded of his fellow former-triumvir. "I still miss him."

As Caesar entered the Curia of Pompey, many eyes turned to him. This wasn't unusual, he was the most powerful man in Rome, more powerful even than the two consuls. "I wonder if it's still necessary to have them elected anymore?" Caesar wondered to himself as he looked around the beautiful building his old ally-turned-enemy had built. "Yes, they are helpful with the administration if nothing else!"

Heavy footfalls from behind made him look around. "Greetings, Caesar," bowed Lucius Cimber, "Do you have time? I have a request."

But Gaius shook his head, "I leave tomorrow, Lucius, I have only a little time today. Whatever it is, it will have to wait until I return."

Pain exploded in his shoulder as something sliced down from behind. Gaius had been a soldier for most of his life, and his training kicked in as he span around. Publius Casca stood before him, a bloody knife in his hand.

"What madness is this?" cried Caesar, pushing Casca away. But looking around, he saw no friendly faces. Rage twisted the glance of every senator there, and as he raised his arms to defend himself, he knew it was no use. "The Ides of March have come..." he whispered to himself.

Brutus was there, and Cassius, and Trebonius, and Basilus, and Aquila, and Galba, and Ligarius, and so many others. So many blades, so many eyes filled with hatred.

The affair was brief, bloody, and brutal. Gasping for breath, the senators backed away from the body lying prone on the floor, their normally pristine togas splatted with red.

The doors of the Curia opened, and more white-robed senators entered. Brutus, his face flushed, turned to greet them. At the front of the new group was Marcus Cicero, his hair greying and his mood somber as he surveyed the scene. "A great day, brothers!" cried Brutus, raising his own bloody knife into the air. "Today we have freed Rome from tyranny!"

Cicero nodded, slowly and gravely. "Yes, but at what cost? I had heard rumors that such a plan was afoot, and yet I could not decide whether to pray for success or failure." He looked down at the bloodied body of Caesar. "I have watched Gaius rise from humble officer to mighty general. I have stood by as he grew in skill and passion. He did great things for us, for Rome, for our people. We should not forget that, even in triumph. But then he changed. He forgot what Rome stands for: limited power; shared responsibility; glory for the city, not the man. And now see what this has brought him. Power corrupts, my friends. And Gaius had absolute power, which corrupted him absolutely. Such a great man, gone. If only he could have stayed as he was: good, honest, passionate, hard-working, and loyal to the city. I weep for him and for Rome, for its brightest star has fallen."

CHARACTER SUMMARY & PRONUNCIATION GUIDE

Gods & Immortals

- Aeolus (Aeolus): God of the winds

- Allecto (Ah-lek-toe): A Fury.

- Apollo (Ap-oll-oh): God of archery and music. Brother of Diana. His name is the same as in Greek.

- Charon (Care-ron): The immortal ferryman who ferries souls to the Underworld.

- Diana (Die-an-ah): Goddess of the hunt and the moon, sister of Apollo. Roman equivalent of Artemis.

- Fates (Fates): The three immortal sisters who spun the tapestry of life and destiny.

- Fury (Fury): An immortal torturer of Pluto's.

- Juno (Ju-no): Queen of the gods, wife of Jupiter. Hates the Trojans and supports the city of Carthage. The Roman version of Hera

- Jupiter (Ju-pit-er): King of the Gods. The Roman version of Zeus.

- Mars (Mars): God of War. The Roman version of Ares. Father of Romulus & Remus.

- Mercury (Mer-cure-ee): The messenger of the gods. The Roman equivalent of Hermes.

- Neptune (Nep-tune): God of the sea. Roman version of Poseidon

- Pluto (Ploo-toe): The god of the Underworld. The Roman equivalent of Hades.

- Venus (Vee-nuss): Goddess of Love, mother of Aeneas. Roman version of Aphrodite.

- Vesta (Ves-ta): Goddess of the hearth and home. Roman equivalent of Hestia.

- Vulcan (Vul-can): The smith god. The Roman equivalent of Hephaistos.

Mortals

- Achilles (Ah-kill-ees): The greatest Greek hero at Troy.

- Aemilius Paullus (Eye-mee-lee-us Paul-lus): A consul of Rome who fought Hannibal at Cannae.

- Aeneas (Ah-knee-as): The demi-god son of the Trojan prince, Anchises, and the goddess of love, Venus.

- Agamemnon (Ag-ah-mem-non): King of Mycenae, led the Greeks to Troy

- Amata (Am-ah-ta): Queen of Latinum, wife of Latinus, mother of Lavinia.

- Amulius (Am-u-lee-uss): Brother of Numitor, from whom he stole the throne of Alba Longa.

- Ancus Marcius (An-cus Mar-cee-uss): Son-in-law of Tullus Hostilius. The fourth king of Rome.

- Aquila (Ah-quill-ah): A senator. One of Caesar's assassins.

- Arcas (Ar-cass): Ancient Arcadian hero.

- Ascanius (As-cay-knee-uss): Son of Aeneas.

- Basilus (Bas-il-us): A senator. One of Caesar's assassins.

- Bibulus (Bib-u-lus): A Roman Politician

- Caenina (Cae-knee-nah): A prince of the Sabines.

- Calpurnia (Cal-purr-nee-ah): Wife of Caesar.

- Carthaginian (Car-th-a-gin-ee-an): An inhabitant of Carthage.

- Cassius Longinus (Cas-see-us Long-ee-us): A senator. One of Caesar's assassins.

- Cato (Cay-toe): A Roman Politician

- Cornelius Sulla (Cor-nee-lee-us Sul-la): An important supporter of Caesar.

- Creusa (Cray-oo-sah): Wife of Aeneas who died at Troy.

- Ctimene (Ce-tie-men-ee): A Trojan woman.

- Dardanus (Dar-dan-uss): An ancient founder of Troy; Aeneas' ancestor.

- Decimus Brutus (Dec-ee-mus Brew-tus): Brother of Marcus Junius Brutus, descendant of Lucius Junius Brutus. A tribune of Caesar.

- Dido (Die-doh): Founding Queen of Carthage.

- Domitius Calvinus (Dom-i-ti-us Cal-vin-uss): An important supporter of Caesar.

- Evander (E-van-derr): King of the Arcadians in Italy.

- Faustulus (Fau-stew-luss): The shepherd who found and raised Romulus and Remus.

- Gaius Claudius Marcellus (Gai-us Claw-dee-uss Mar-cell-uss): A consul of Rome

- Gaius Flaminius (Guy-uss Flam-in-ee-uss): A consul of Rome who fought Hannibal at The Battle of Lake Trasimene

- Gaius Julius Caesar (Guy-uss Ju-lee-uss Cee-sar): One of Rome's greatest Roman generals. Member of the first triumvirate.

- Galba (Gal-bah): A senator. One of Caesar's assassins.

- Gnaeus Pompey (G-nai-uss Pom-pee): One of Rome's greatest Roman generals. Member of the first triumvirate.

- Hamilcar Barca (Ham-ill-car Bar-kah): A Carthaginian general and statesman, father of Hannibal, Hasdrubal, and Mago.

- Hannibal (Han-knee-bal): The greatest Carthaginian General. Son of Hamilcar. Brother of Mago and Hasdrubal.

- Hasdrubal (Has-drew-bal): Brother of Hannibal Barca

- Hector (Hek-tor): Prince of Troy, son of Priam, the Trojan's greatest warrior. Slain by Achilles.

- Hersilia (Her-sil-ee-ah): A Sabine woman. Romulus' wife, the first queen of Rome.

- Hesione (Hess-ee-oh-knee): Sister of Priam, king of Troy.

- Iarbas (Ee-yar-bass): A king in Africa.

- Labienus (Lab-i-en-uss): Pompey's cavalry commander.

- Latinus (Lat-ee-nuss): King of Latinum, Italy.

- Lavinia (Lah-vin-ee-ah): Daughter of Latinus.

- Ligarius (Lie-gar-ee-us): A senator. One of Caesar's assassins.

- Lucius Cimber (Lu-cee-us Cim-berr): A senator. One of Caesar's assassins.

- Lucius Cornellius Lentulus (Cor-nee-lee-us Len-tu-luss): A consul of Rome

- Lucius Junius Brutus (Lu-cee-us Jun-ee-uss Brew-tus): A senator who ousted the last king of Rome, Tarquin the Proud.

- Lycaon (Ly-cah-on): Ancient Arcadian hero.

- Mago (Mah-go): Brother of Hannibal Barca

- Marcus Antonius (Mar-cus An-tone-ee-us): An important supporter of Caesar.

- Marcus Cornelius (Mar-cus Cor-knee-lee-uss): An early Roman leader.

- Marcus Junius Brutus (Mar-cus Jun-ee-uss Brew-tus): Brother of Decimus Brutus, a descendant of Lucius Junius Brutus. A senior senator.

- Marcus Licinius Crassus (Mar-cus Lick-in-ee-us Crass-us): One of Rome's greatest Roman generals. Rome's richest man. Member of the first triumvirate.

- Marcus Tullius Cicero (Mar-cus Tul-le-uss Kick-ker-row): A Roman senator, possibly the greatest Roman orator and statesman.

- Minos (My-noss): King of Crete.

- Minucius Rufus (Min-u-kee-us Rue-fus): A Roman senator and rival of Fabius.

- Numa Pompilius (New-ma Pom-pil-ee-us): A Sabine, the second king of Rome.

- Numitor (Nu-mit-or): Grandfather of Romulus and Remus, the rightful king of Alba Longa.

- Octavian (Oc-tay-vee-an): Adopted son of Caesar. The future first emperor of Rome.

- Odysseus (Oh-dee-see-uss): The smartest, most cunning Greek hero at Troy.

- Pallas (Pal-ass): Prince of Arcadia, son of Evander.

- Priam (Pry-am): King of Troy, father of Hector

- Publius Casca (Pub-lee-us Cas-cah): A senator. One of Caesar's assassins.

- Publius Cornelius Scipio (Pub-lee-us-Cor-nee-lee-us Skip-ee-oh): A Roman general who defeated Hannibal. Known thereafter as Scipio Africanus.

- Quintus Fabius Maximus (Quin-tus Fay-be-uss Max-ee-mus): A distinguished Roman politician and consul multiple times. Elected Dictator to deal with Hannibal.

- Remus (Re-muss): Son of Mars and Rhea Silvia. Twin brother of Romulus.

- Rhea Silvia (Ray-ah Sil-vee-ah): Mother of Romulus and Remus.

- Romulus (Rom-u-luss): Son of Mars and Rhea Silvia. Twin brother of Remus, founder of Rome.

- Rutulii (Ru-tu-lee-ee): The descendants of the Rutulians, a tribe of Italy.

- Sabine (Say-bine): An Italian Tribe.

- Scipio Africanus (Scip-ee-oh Af-ree-can-uss): A Roman senator and general - Full name Publius Cornelius Scipio.

- Sempronius Longus (Sem-pro-nee-us Long-us): A consul of Rome who fought Hannibal at The Battle of the Trebia

- Spartacus (Spar-ta-cuss): A gladiator who led a rebellion.

- Spurius Carvilius (Spur-ee-us Car-vil-ee-us): A consul of Rome who had Fabius elected dictator.

- Sybil (Si-bill): A prophetess from Cumae, Italy.

- Tarquin (Tar-quin) "The Proud": The seventh and last king of Rome.

- Terentius Varro (Ter-en-tee-us Varro): A consul of Rome who fought Hannibal at Cannae.

- Teucris (T-yoo-criss): An ancient founder of Troy; Aeneas' ancestor.

- Theseus (Thee-see-uss): Son of Aegeus of Athens, slayer of the Minotaur.

- Titus Tatius (Tie-tus Tay-tious): King of the Sabines

- Trebonius (Trey-bon-ee-us): A senator. One of Caesar's assassins.

- Tullus Hostilius (Tul-lus Hos-til-ee-uss): Nephew of Numa Pompilius. The third king of Rome.

- Turnus (Turn-uss): Prince of the Rutulians, an enemy of Aeneas.

- Tyrian (Tee-ree-an): A Carthaginian noble, an advisor of Dido.

- Vibius Tatius (Vib-ee-us Tay-tious): A leading Sabine

Places

- Alba Longa (Al-ba Long-ah): A city founded by Ascanius, son of Aeneas.

- Alps (Al-ps): The mountain range at the top of Italy.

- Arcadia (Ar-cay-dee-ah): A city built where Rome now stands.

- Aventine (Av-en-tine): One of the seven hills of Rome.

- Cannae (Can-ay): A spot on the eastern coast of Italy, where Hannibal destroyed a much larger Roman army.

- Capitoline (Cap-i-toe-line): One of the seven hills of Rome.

- Carrhae (Car-hai): A place in Turkey, where Crassus died.

- Carthage (Car-th-age): A city on the northern coast of Africa, founded by Queen Dido.

- Crete (Creet): The largest and southern-most island of the Greece archipelago.

- Cumae (Cu-may): A small town near Rome.

- Cures (Cure-res): A small town near Rome.

- Curia of Pompey (Cure-ree-ah): A meeting hall in Rome built by Pompey.

- Delos (Dell-oss): An island sacred to Apollo, where his prophetic priestess lived.

- Egypt (Ee-gypt): A country in north Africa.

- Enipeus (En-ee-pee-us): A river in Greece.

- Field of Mars (Mars): A wide, open area just on the outskirts of old Rome, where the army trained and elections were held.

- Gaul (G-all): Modern France, but the provinces stretched down over the Alps into northern Italy.

- Iberia (I-beer-ee-ah): Modern Spain

- Ilipa (Ill-ee-pah): A plain in the south of Spain.

- Latinum (Lat-ee-num): Home of Latinus, a city near the western coast of Italy.

- Libya (Lib-ee-ah): Area on the northern coast of Africa.

- Lugdunum (Lug-dun-um): Modern Lyon, France.

- Mediterranean (Med-ee-ter-an-ee-an): The sea lying between Europe and Africa.

- Mount Dogantzis (Dog-ant-ziss): A mountain at Pharsalus, Greece.

- Mycenae (My-see-knee): Home of Agamemnon

- Numidia (New-mid-ee-ah): An area in north Africa.

- Olympus (Oh-lim-puss): Mountain in Greece, where the Gods lived.

- Palatine (Pal-a-tine): One of the seven hills of Rome. Romulus' favorite.

- Parthia (Par-thee-ah): An empire to the east of Rome.

- Pharsalus (Phar-sa-luss): A place in central Greece.

- Pillars of Hercules (Her-cu-lees): The Strait of Gibraltar.

- Rubicon (Rue-bi-con): A river in Italy which marked the northern boundary between the provinces of Italia and Gaul.

- Rutulia (Ru-tu-lee-ah): Home of Turnus, a neighbor of Latinum.

- Saguntum (Sag-un-tum): A town in Iberia in Carthaginin-ian lands, but allied with Rome.

- Sicily (Si-ci-lee): A large island in the south of Italy.

- Tarpeian Rock (Tar-pay-an): An outcrop in Rome.

- Temple of Janus (Jan-uss): A temple of the two-faced god of door-ways. Remained closed except when Rome was at war.

- Tiber (Tie-ber): Also a god. The river of Rome.

- Trasimene (Tras-ee-main): A lake in the center of Italy.

- Trebia (Tray-be-ah): A river in northern Italy.

- Troy (Tr-oi): A great city on the edge of Asia, the site of the 10-year long war.

- Tyre (Ty-ree): Dido's homeland.

- Underworld (Un-der-world): The land of the dead, ruled by Pluto.

- Zama (Zah-mah): A plain in north Africa just outside Carthage.

Miscellaneous

- Adirim (Ad-ir-im): The Carthaginian ruling council, equivalent to the Roman Senate.

- Auxiliary (Aux-ill-ar-ree): A supporting soldier in the Roman legion, usually an archer, slinger, or light horseman.

- consul (con-sul): The most senior magistracy in Rome. Two governed together for a year, sharing power and leading armies.

- dictator (dic-tay-tor): An emergency Roman magistracy - had total power for just 6 months.

- forum (for-rum): The economic and political area of Rome.

- Imperator (Im-per-ah-tor): A Roman General, literally "he who commands".

- interrex (in-ter-rex): An interim magistracy in Rome after the death of Romulus.

- laurel crown (lau-rell): A crown of laurel leaves which a triumphant general could wear.

- legion (lee-gee-on): The Roman army, a force of anywhere between 5,000 and 10,000 men.

- legionary (lee-gee-on-air-ree): A Roman soldier.

- Minotaur (My-no-tor): A monster with the head of a bull and the body of a man.

- Republic (Ree-pub-lick): The political system whereby Rome was ruled by an elected council.

- Senate (Sen-ate): The ruling council of Rome, made up of the wisest and most experienced men of the state.

- senator (sen-a-tor): A member of the Roman Senate

- Sufetes (Su-fe-tes): The senior magistrates in Carthage, equivalent of the Roman consuls.

- toga (to-ga): Traditional Roman clothing for the upper classes, a huge expanse of cloth draped carefully around the wearer.

- tribune (tri-bune): A junior officer in the army. Also a junior magistracy in the senate.

- Triumph (Try-um-ph): A great procession through Rome to celebrate a returning, triumphant general.

- Triumvirate(Tri-um-vir-ate): An informal political alliance between three men.

- Vestal Virgin (Vest-al Vir-gin): A priestess in Rome, sworn to keep the "eternal flame" burning.

BITE-SIZE TIMELESS TALES COLLECTIONS!

Made in the USA
Middletown, DE
04 November 2024

63857005R00096